MOUNTAIN PITFALL

Fargo had scant time to react when he rode smack into the ingenious trap. But everything seemed to happen in slowed-down nightmare time. He had encountered this "trip-and-pit" set-up before the Ovaro went down hard, hurling Fargo straight over the saddle horn and into the pitfall. The Ovaro almost tumbled in on top of his master, crushing him, but barely avoided it with a powerful twist that threw the stallion to one side of the trap, safe from falling.

Fargo's feet crashed through the camouflaged cover, and he immediately spotted the sharpened wooden stakes, their poisoned tips glistening black in the moonlight. Only a fraction of a second before that row of stakes would have impaled him, Fargo made a desperate, reckless bid to cheat the reaper. He managed to brace his feet against one dirt wall of the pit and push off hard, just barely clearing the poisoned spears. But the move left him off balance with no time to brace for impact before he slammed hard, head and left shoulder first, into the dirt just behind the stakes.

He felt a mule-kick impact, saw a bright orange starburst inside his skull, and then Skye Fargo's world shut down to silence and darkness.

THE TRAILSMAN
#265

DAKOTA
DEATH RATTLE

by

Jon Sharpe

A SIGNET BOOK

SIGNET
Published by New American Library, a division of
Penguin Group (USA) Inc., 375 Hudson Street,
New York, New York 10014, U.S.A.
Penguin Books Ltd, 80 Strand,
London WC2R 0RL, England
Penguin Books Australia Ltd, 250 Camberwell Road,
Camberwell, Victoria 3124, Australia
Penguin Books Canada Ltd, 10 Alcorn Avenue,
Toronto, Ontario, Canada M4V 3B2
Penguin Books (N.Z.) Ltd, Cnr Rosedale and Airborne Roads,
Albany, Auckland 1310, New Zealand

Penguin Books Ltd, Registered Offices:
80 Strand, London WC2R 0RL, England

First published by Signet, an imprint of New American Library,
a division of Penguin Group (USA) Inc.

First Printing, November 2003
10 9 8 7 6 5 4 3 2 1

The first chapter of this book previously appeared in *Snake River Ruins,* the two
hundred sixty-fourth volume in this series.

Copyright © Penguin Group (USA) Inc., 2003
All rights reserved

 REGISTERED TRADEMARK—MARCA REGISTRADA

Printed in the United States of America

PUBLISHER'S NOTE
This is a work of fiction. Names, characters, places, and incidents either are the
product of the author's imagination or are used fictitiously, and any resemblance
to actual persons, living or dead, events, or locales is entirely coincidental.

The Trailsman

Beginnings . . . they bend the tree and they mark the man. Skye Fargo was born when he was eighteen. Terror was his midwife, vengeance his first cry. Killing spawned Skye Fargo, ruthless, cold-blooded murder. Out of the acrid smoke of gunpowder still hanging in the air, he rose, cried out a promise never forgotten.

The Trailsman they began to call him all across the West: searcher, scout, hunter, the man who could see where others only looked, his skills for hire but not his soul, the man who lived each day to the fullest, yet trailed each tomorrow. Skye Fargo, the Trailsman, the seeker who could take the wildness of a land and the wanting of a woman and make them his own.

Black Hills, Dakota Territory, 1859—
Where the ancient laws of the Manitus demand blood,
and the deadliest disease of all is gold fever.

1

Overhead, vultures wheeled like merchants of death against a mother-of-pearl morning sky, warning the bearded, buckskin-clad rider that trouble lurked just beyond the next ridge.

Skye Fargo nudged the riding thong from the hammer of his Colt, easing back on the reins to halt the Ovaro. They had just rounded the shoulder of Ragged Top Mountain, well up toward the summit. Now Fargo's lake-blue eyes enjoyed an excellent view of the pine-covered slopes overlooking Spearfish Canyon, bright with splashes of larkspur, daisies, and other wild flowers. A red-tailed hawk soared on a wind current, and here and there among the darkly forested slopes huge chunks of crystallized gypsum flashed in the sunlight. The air was thinner up here, and Fargo felt slightly lightheaded.

White men called these forested mountains the Black Hills, Sioux called them the *Paha Sapa*. By any name, Fargo considered them one of the great natural surprises of the American West. They formed a virtual island of timber surrounded by level, barren, treeless plain. It was not as arid here as in the surrounding Dakota Territory because some of the peaks rose more than a mile high. They arrested rain clouds that otherwise quickly blew over the dry plains. Thus these mountains had become a haven for grizzly bears and other wildlife.

Despite their natural beauty and good hunting, however, Fargo normally avoided the Black Hills like he would the mouth of hell. Those wheeling vultures just ahead of him now were not an uncommon sight here.

These mountains were surrounded by Sioux and Northern Cheyennes, no tribes to mess with. And the Sioux, especially strong just west and south of these disputed mountains, were particularly determined to keep gold-

1

seeking white men out of the *Paha Sapa*. They considered this unique plains oasis the sacred center of their universe.

Fargo knew the Sioux had no legal claim recognized by white men's courts, just squatter's rights. But they were being challenged in the Platte Valley to the south and were determined to keep these sacred mountains free of whiteskins. Fargo saw their side of the matter, too, and had not planned to intrude.

He had been carefully skirting the Black Hills, on his way north to the Yellowstone country. But two youthful Sioux braves, probably looking to earn their first coup feather, had stolen his horse while he was afoot hunting for game. He had been forced to track them east into the *Paha Sapa*. He stole the Ovaro back without harming either Indian, and now all Fargo wanted was to put this wondrous but troublesome place behind him. Too many fools had come here looking for gold and found only an early grave.

And once again, apparently, danger lay over the next ridge, threatening to snarl his peaceful plans. Fargo kneed the Ovaro forward, seeking low seams. From long habit he avoided the crests of ridges, knowing the swales behind them were favorite lairs of bushwhackers.

Fargo whiffed the scalp-tingling smell of death even before he spotted any actual trouble. A steady buzzing noise increased as they advanced. Soon, huge blowflies annoyed the Ovaro and kept him snorting and flipping his head.

When the stallion began to resist, stutter-stepping sideways, Fargo reined in. He swung his leg over the cantle and dismounted, landing light as a cat. He was tall and rangy, much of his weather-bronzed face shadowed by the slanted brim of his hat. He slid his Henry from its saddle boot and left the reins dangling, knowing his well-trained Ovaro would not wander. Holding the Henry at a high port, he proceeded down the tree-covered slope on foot, leap-frogging from pine to pine as he advanced.

He glanced through a break in the trees and spotted a little clearing carpeted with bluebonnets. Then he looked closer and also recognized pale human flesh lying among the lush grass and wild flowers. Five, no—six bodies, all men, stripped naked and apparently lifeless. Some were covered in a shifting, dark blanket of flies.

Fargo felt that familiar quickening of his senses, but remained calm and focused. Confident but careful, that's how a man endured on the frontier. He studied the surrounding trees for several minutes. Birds of every sort serenaded him from countless limbs—a reassuring sign that men were not hiding close by. Nonetheless, he turned sideways to reduce the target for any hidden marksmen when he started across the little clearing.

A sudden voice, quavering and weak, froze him in place like a hound on point.

"God sakes, don't come no closer, mister! I'm a gone-up case. We . . . we all are. It's mountain fever."

Fargo was still about fifteen feet away from the first body. He spotted one fever-flushed, glassy-eyed face watching him. At the dying man's words, he felt a cold sweat break out on his temples. Of all the killers on the frontier, none was more fearsome than the silent horseman called pestilence.

The man's chest heaved as he tried to suck air into his fluid-filled lungs.

"Too . . . too late now for medicine," he rasped. "They deliberately kept us from a doc."

"Who did? How'd you fellers end up all alone down here?" Fargo asked.

"Forced . . . forced at gun point by strangers," the man gasped out. "We're all prospectors. Had . . . had us a claim west of here in Wyoming. Fever hit our camp. A few days later three hired guns showed up, forced a bunch of us . . . forced us to put on brand . . . brand-spanking new clothes. Then they herded us into a wagon and hauled us . . . here into the Black Hills. Paid some half-breed to strip the clothes back off us and fold 'em up again."

"What happened to the clothes after that?"

But a coughing spasm interrupted the dying man's narrative. Fargo had never had mountain fever, but knew it was fatal if not treated in time. He also knew he was susceptible now. But sympathy roiled his guts when the man begged for water. He hurried back to the Ovaro and grabbed his bull's-eye canteen off the saddle horn.

However, it was too late. By the time he returned, the unfortunate sourdough was giving up the ghost.

"Just stay back, mister, I can't swallow nothing anyhow. Don't bother . . . burying us," he managed to rasp out on a

3

final breath. "Touching us will—will only kill you. Them . . . goldang vultures'll take care of . . . the remains."

There was a phlegmy rattle, like pebbles caught in a sluice gate, as the miner's lungs expelled their long, final breath. Fargo had seen death more often than most men, but it never got any easier to watch. He moved quickly around the clearing, verifying that no one else was alive. These men had suffered terribly, deserted and exposed to the elements, and Fargo felt sympathy and anger warring within him. Nor could he help wondering about those "brand-spanking new clothes" and just who they were intended to infect.

He couldn't bury the men, warning or no, because he had no shovel. But Fargo was damned if he'd let those vultures feast, leaving eyeless, flesh-scoured skulls as the final indignity. He spent the better part of an hour scrambling down to nearby Spearfish Creek, returning with boulders and heaping them over the bodies. It was a humble tomb, perhaps, but the best he could manage.

"God have mercy on their poor souls," he muttered, hat in hand, before he returned to his horse.

Even the lowest sinner didn't deserve to die that hard. Yet clearly someone intended to deliberately spread the disease.

Fargo slid his Henry back into its boot, then stepped into a stirrup and swung aboard. He tugged rein and clucked to the Ovaro, heading back up toward the old supply trail he'd been following above, on easier terrain. He was in the northern tip of the Black Hills and planned to keep Spearfish Creek in sight until he emerged out on the surrounding plains. The sooner the better.

"If I owned hell and the Black Hills," he muttered to his horse, revising a remark he'd once heard an army officer make about Texas, "I'd rent out the Black Hills and live in hell."

The rough trail was sandy and rocky, with washouts that had to be laboriously detoured. Fargo was forced to dismount often and lead the Ovaro through dense thickets or across shale-littered slopes. At one point, just as he emerged from a thick, tangled deadfall bristling with thorns,

4

the metallic snick of a rifle hammer being cocked halted him in his tracks.

"Hold it right there, mister. Make any quick moves, I'll put daylight through you."

Two men stepped out from the screening timber on both sides of the trail ahead. Their occupation was immediately obvious from the red clay and dark ore stains splattering their clothing and footgear. The prospector who had just spoken was a thickset man who looked strong as horse radish, with wind-cracked lips and a huge soup-strainer mustache. He wore a pair of new overalls. But it was his long .54 caliber Jennings rifle that got most of Fargo's attention.

"Getcher right hand away from that belt gun!" the man's companion snapped. He was a younger, thinner version of the man with the Jennings except that he aimed an old cap-and-ball dragoon pistol at Fargo's vitals. "Hollis Blackburn must be gettin' confident now, sending only one hired gun to do his dirty work."

"Lower them widow makers, boys," Fargo replied calmly. "I never heard of any Hollis Blackburn."

"That won't spend, mister," the prospector with the Jennings growled. "If you *ain't* one of Blackburn's gunslicks, how's come you got this far and you're still alive? Now, you just turn back around and go tell him we don't spit when he says hawk."

Fargo knew, better than most, the West was harsh. But he also knew that most men meant no harm. These two were scared, not criminal.

"Gunslick?" he repeated. "Look close at my rig. Notice the rear sight ain't filed off my short iron, nor the trigger guard cut away. And my holster ain't tied down low. What kind of gunslick do I amount up to?"

The two men exchanged glances at this logic, doubt easing some of the hostility off their faces.

"Well, don't tell us you aim to roost here?" the older one said. "You ain't got the look of a sourdough."

"And how do we know," chimed in the other, "you ain't riding the owl hoot trail?"

Fargo laughed outright. "Would a sane man on the dodge flee *into* the Black Hills? I'd sooner take my chances

5

with a white starpacker than a Sioux war party. I'm only here because two young bucks relieved me of my horse and I had to steal him back."

"You know, Elijah," the younger man remarked to his companion, "this jay looks more like a mountain man or an army scout than a hired gun-thrower. He don't spend much time in rented rooms, that's for sure."

He thumbed the dragoon pistol back to half cock and lowered it.

"Call me Pow," he told Fargo. "It's bobtail for Powhatan. Powhatan Stone. This here is my big brother Elijah."

Elijah hitched his sagging denims. "Beg pardon for the rough reception, Mister? . . ."

"Fargo. Skye Fargo."

Recognition glinted in both men's eyes.

"Sure! You're the jasper some call the Trailsman," Elijah said. "Not so long back, there was a shooting scrape twixt you and the Danford gang just east of here in the Badlands. Step forward a piece, Mr. Fargo. There's something you oughta see 'fore you go any farther."

The brothers led him about twenty feet ahead to a spot where the tall pine trees had been cleared for lumber. This opened a clear view of the canyon below and a sprawling, ramshackle mining camp. The timber-denuded slopes below them bristled with tar-papered shacks and clapboard she-bangs, tents, and even some crude brush shanties. Some of the better-constructed dwellings boasted windows with panes of oiled paper. Fargo spotted a portable windmill for driving drinking water to a common well and pump. The prospectors had diverted creek water with ditches and brush dams to grow foodstuffs around their dwellings.

"Welcome to Busted Hump. Population about one hundred and fifty souls, though that number is dwindling. Don't look like much, mebbe, but that place represented a dream to us once," Elijah said with evident pride. "Oh, nobody's been pulling out any fist-size nuggets. But you can still pan gold right out of the creek gravel. Why, with just a pan and a sluice box, a man can earn a living wage and be his own boss."

"But now?" Pow cut in, his tone bitter. "Now it's just a God-forgotten hellhole."

Fargo had his own contrary notions about the "dream"

represented by gold fever. By 1859 most prospectors had deserted California's depleted gold fields for Nevada's rich Comstock Lode. Colorado, and recently Idaho, were also swarming with new prospectors. Far from going out, the fires of America's get-rich-quick fever were burning hotter than ever.

If it happened in California, the editorialists were urging, why not rich gold strikes elsewhere? Soldiers, farmers, clerks, school teachers—everywhere men were deserting their jobs, even their families, lured by the promise of wealth.

"I can tell from your face," Elijah said, "that you think we're fools to be here, what with Sioux Indians in these hills as thick as fleas on a hound."

"You ain't fools," Fargo gainsaid. "Any man has a right to seek his fortune honestly. But for every man who hits a bonanza, a hundred more come up with nothing but the sniffles. Meantime, the Sioux are boiling mad and painted for battle."

The gold rumors had persisted ever since an early Jesuit missionary hinted he had seen evidence of it in the Black Hills. Early trappers swore they met Indians using gold-tipped arrows. A reported strike in 1834 ended in disaster with Sioux killing all the miners. Another party in 1852 found gold but had to flee before taking any out.

"Anyhow," Elijah said, "it ain't the Sioux that's been our worst enemy."

Fargo's eyes were trained to read details, and he could fill in some of what Elijah left unspoken. Down below, among the gullies washed red with eroded soil, he could see dark patches where gun powder had been burned over fresh graves to discourage predators.

His eyes shifted to a building of notched logs, set off away from the rest of camp. It was new and hastily erected.

"That's a pesthouse, ain't it?" he inquired.

Elijah nodded glumly. "As if we ain't got us enough troubles, mountain fever has just hit our camp. We got sixteen people sick already, some of 'em women and kids. Last I heard, that problem hadn't got no farther east than the Front Range in Colorado."

Fargo's gaze cut to the new blue overalls both brothers wore. "Sometimes problems move—or *get* moved. Have

7

you folks recently had a shipment of goods come in—including new clothing?"

Elijah frowned. "'Bout three days ago, matter fact. Why?"

Fargo explained his encounter with the dying Wyoming prospector. Both brothers paled at the news.

"Hollis Blackburn, that son of a whore," Pow swore with quiet anger. "He musta somehow had them infected duds slipped in with the rest of our shipment."

"Who is this Hollis Blackburn?" Fargo asked.

"He's a snake-eyed British bastard who'd swipe the coppers from a dead man's eyes, that's who. Calls himself an 'agent' for the Alliance Mining Company," Elijah supplied. "Which means he's the murdering dirt-worker for a gang of foreign and Eastern investors who back giant mining operations—the strip miners, the hardrock blasters, the hydraulic operations that wash entire mountains into gravel heaps."

Fargo nodded. He remembered seeing the Alliance Mining Company's clearly posted signs a few miles back from here: WARNING! TRESPASSERS WILL BE SHOT AT AND IF MISSED WILL BE PROSECUTED!

"He's got a mining engineer's report that says Busted Hump sits smack over a rich gold vein just above the bedrock," Elijah added. "We're small potatoes. It's what's *under* our claims he's after."

He pointed at the surrounding pine slopes. "He keeps a bunch of hard tails on his payroll. They're dug in deeper than ticks on a shaggy buffalo. Doing all they can to starve us out of here. We had some good butcher beef until they somehow slipped poisoned grain to our stock. They've even poisoned the local water holes with strychnine to thin out the game hereabouts. Hell, we're boiling old hides to make soup. We're down to our last salt meat now and whatever fish we can pull from the creek."

"With plenty of air pudding for dessert," Pow chimed in sarcastically. "And since the only law here in the Dakota Territory is lynch law, ain't thing one we can do about it. Us prospectors got the endurance of a doorknob, but we're poor shakes as gunmen."

"Now they've gone and infected our camp with fever," Elijah summed up. "And all we got for a 'doctor' is a quack who sells worthless patent medicines, maybe pulls a tooth now and then. Worse, we can't get through to Shoshone Falls to get a real doc. Blackburn's gun-throwers got all the trails covered, and besides, we had to eat our last good horse."

"Shoshone Falls," Fargo repeated. "That a town?"

"Town? Hell, it's a bull-and-bear pit," Elijah assured him. "Due south from here, just past Thunderhead Mountain. But they got a real doctor there and a good mercantile."

"It's a damn long chance," Pow admitted, "but the only one we got. Way we figure, if we don't get some medicine in about three days, a good number of us are done for. We need other supplies, too, need 'em bad. It's only about thirty-five miles to Thunderhead Mountain. But it's a rough piece of landscape, made even rougher by Hollis Blackburn's jobbers. They're watchin' us right now, and they'll know that any rider going south is going for help. They'll make it hot for him."

While he listened to all this, Fargo had whistled the Ovaro forward. He opened a saddlebag and pulled out a slab of salt pork wrapped in cheesecloth, handing it to Elijah.

"Just slice it thin and fry it up good," he told the brothers. "It's mean grub and chews like tree bark. I only eat it when I can't tag fresh game. But it'll help tide your camp until I get back with a doc and some supplies."

"Get back?" Elijah echoed. "*You're* gonna risk that trip for strangers?"

"Once a man tells me his name," Fargo said as he stirruped and swung up onto the hurricane deck, "he ain't a stranger, is he? Besides, 'pears I got the only good horse, and I'd rather ride him than eat him."

"It won't be no stroll through the roses," Pow warned him.

"I'm one to give as good as I get," Fargo assured him as he tugged his pinto around. "You fellows hunker down and keep your powder dry. This fandango's just now getting started, and before it's over things will get mighty lively around here, count on it."

2

In times of danger from ambush, Skye Fargo usually preferred the high ground. For now, as he bore due south toward Thunderhead Mountain, he had it.

He was up so high now that only a few wind-twisted jack pines clung to the flinty summits just above him—scant cover for any hidden shooters. But the timber-thick slope below him posed a constant threat. His eyes scanned it continuously, searching for the glint of sunshine on weapons.

Dust rose under the Ovaro's hoofs, swirled in the high-altitude gusts, then settled to powder the trailside brush. Even up this high, cherries and gooseberries grew so thick, in places he could pluck them from horseback. Clouds tended to gather quickly over these isolated Dakota peaks, and lightning danger was constant even on sunny days.

He watched a peregrine falcon soar gracefully overhead, then suddenly dive on an unsuspecting rabbit. Its death squeals were a blunt reminder that these mountains teemed with predators of all sorts. He recalled that dying prospector's last, struggling breath, thought again about how much those six men had suffered, left alone to die slow and hard.

And now the residents of Busted Hump were in the same danger. All because of this damned gold fever—another deadly disease, one that was sweeping the nation.

Fargo had no proof that this fellow Hollis Blackburn was behind the deliberate spreading of mountain fever. But *some*body sure's hell was, and if he found proof of who it was, that somebody was marked for a bullet or a gallows limb.

At one point the trail took a switchbacking loop, and soon Fargo had an excellent view of the surrounding plains below. It was due north from here, on the northern bank of the Missouri near where it joined the Yellowstone, that he'd been headed before fate intervened. The site of Fort

Union, the biggest trading post on the Great Plains, built by the American Fur Company.

But those heady days of Manuel Lisa's great fur-trading empire had given way to railroad and mining ventures and the new class of "speculators." Rich foreigners and folks back east who profited off other men's risk and hard work without forsaking the comfort of their gaslights and feather beds.

Even as Fargo ruminated on these troubling changes, he rounded another bend and confronted more proof that no place in the West was safe from the reckless profiteers: acres and acres of mountain slope that had been stripped bare of timber. In no time at all, that entire slope would become a worthless, ugly erosion scar.

He had passed this stretch earlier, the area posted with NO TRESPASSING signs. The Alliance Mining Company had no doubt felled those trees to timber the stopes in their underground mining operation. The mine area itself was still out of sight from here, located far below in Spearfish Canyon. A razorback ridge blocked it from view.

But why, he wondered, had he encountered no trouble so far? The Stone brothers swore that thugs for the mining company controlled this area. Perhaps the brothers were coloring up the facts a mite, as frontier types were wont to do. Or maybe the thugs had dismissed one lone rider, obviously not a miner or prospector, as no threat to their interests.

However, Fargo assumed nothing and stayed alert. The trail took an abrupt drop of a few hundred yards, a necessary detour past a steep, rock-strewn slope, clearly unstable: tons of granite boulders and talus rock on the verge of giving way under its own weight. It lay to Fargo's left and rose sharply above him. To his right, just off the narrow trail, a steep limestone cliff dropped in a sheer plunge of at least five hundred feet.

The Ovaro didn't like this stretch any better than Fargo did. As he had the first time they passed this way, the stallion resisted the bit. Fargo patted the Ovaro's neck to calm him.

"Straight ahead, old campaigner, just keep up the strut. We'll be past it in two shakes."

Man and horse were almost halfway past the rock-strewn

slope when an ear-splitting detonation, straight above them, made the Ovaro rear up, nickering in fright. Fargo was forced to grab the pommel in one hand to keep from sliding off the saddle. He recognized the air-thumping concussion of a huge powder charge.

The slope, inert one moment, suddenly seemed to come to life like a huge, angry gray beast shaking itself awake. Before Fargo could even get the Ovaro calm again, those tons of rock and scree were hurtling down toward them with all the destructive fury of Judgment Day.

"That explosion just now, Mitt," Hollis Blackburn said to his mine captain. "Is it what I think it is?"

Mitt Brennan had just ridden into the center of the well-organized mining camp and still sat astride his handsome sorrel gelding. As for Blackburn, only moments earlier he had emerged from the assay shack where gold dust was tested by washing it in acid, then mixing it with mercury. In the background an ore wagon with high wheels was setting out for the company smelter in Spearfish. The double teams of mules were so long the driver rode the lead mule.

"Sure is, Mr. Blackburn," Brennan replied. "Whoever that stranger on the pinto stallion was, he's worm fodder now. We just—"

"I know who he is," Blackburn interrupted. "And more important, I know his reputation. He's a damned Robin Hood in buckskins—precisely the *wrong* man to have in these parts after the bone-headed blunder Orrin and Boyd pulled. I thought you assured me you had your subordinates well in hand?"

Brennan swung down, whistling to a Chinese worker to take his horse. Despite his job title as mine captain, Brennan wore range clothes and a dusty neckerchief. He was a long-jawed man with a thin, sharp-nosed face and old small-pox scars marring his features.

"Boyd and Orrin usually follow orders," he protested. "So does Cas. But, see, they couldn't leave the sick prospectors behind because there wasn't nobody who'd touch the damn infected clothes until—"

Blackburn silenced him by raising one hand.

"Mitt, I've told you before," he admonished in his crisp British accent, "it isn't necessary, is it, to tell me everything? That's why I hire supposedly good men—to take care of the troublesome details."

When it came to breaking the law, Blackburn always issued indirect orders and stopped his hirelings from telling him too much. He had excellent legal training, having once been a barrister in London.

He stood out, among this rough-and-tumble group of miners and hired thugs, like a rhinestone vest. His waxed mustache was neatly trimmed and twirled, and he wore a vermilion ranch suit and expensive hand-tooled boots. His calling cards, printed on expensive pebbled stock, identified him as a businessman's troubleshooter. A diamond belt buckle and the genuine pearl snaps on his cuffs proved he was a man known for pleasing his employers.

His current employer was known simply as the Alliance, since its investors were all international speculators. Mitt Brennan's chief job consisted of terrorizing and intimidating the Alliance miners into submission to brutal work conditions. Hollis had an even larger job: clearing the profit path of any and *all* encumbrances. As a respectable cover for this task, he was called Mine Supervisor.

In truth, Hollis Blackburn was a callow and ruthless man who fooled the decent with educated talk and fancy tailoring. He had arrived in America fifteen years earlier and immediately purchased enough slaves to make a cotton fortune in the rich black soil of east Texas. But he had squandered it gambling, and now he stood to make it back if he could clear up certain troubles for the Alliance Mining Company. But time was pressing in on him.

"Well, anyhow," Brennan said, "there ain't no way in hell anybody on the trail could have escaped that rockslide in time."

"You *saw* him get trapped? You'd swear to that?"

Brennan frowned. "Hell, how could I? Once that charge went off, all you could see was dust. But that rider is buried deep now, you can take *that* to the bank."

Hollis crimped a paper and shook some tobacco into it. He felt a deep contempt for Brennan and the rest of these uncouth American ruffians, ungrammatical men unfamiliar with opera houses and good grooming. But he believed that money was like manure—it worked best when it was spread around. Thus, he had no qualms about paying his thugs well to do whatever was required to please his principals, as he called the wealthy investors who employed him.

"No, Mitt, correction: I *cannot* take your assurances to the bank," he reminded his hireling. "The problem to be solved is really quite simple. There's too many pigs for the teats. And you had better make it crystal clear to Cas, Boyd, and Orrin—I shan't wait indefinitely while they twiddle their thumbs. I want this situation with Busted Hump resolved, and resolved bloody soon. Time is a bird, my friend, and the bird is on the wing. Besides the fever situation, how goes the campaign?"

"Well, Cas and Boyd just finished—"

"Skip the incriminating details," Blackburn reminded him. "Speak in generalities."

"Yeah, sorry. *Some*body musta tore out that brush dam on Spearfish Creek. The lower diggings at Busted Hump are now flooded."

"Crying shame," Blackburn murmured with effortless hypocrisy. "How much more can those poor prospectors endure?"

Hollis Blackburn was a claim jumper on a massive scale. He wasn't out to acquire just one man's diggings, but the entire area of Busted Hump. His employers had paid a huge sum to bring a team of experts out and do underground surveying. The entire area under Busted Hump was laced with rich veins of ore. In fact he had one of the rock samples in his pocket right now—he could actually *see* the rich threads of gold in it.

"Ah, them sourdoughs are all gurgle and no guts," Brennan scoffed. "Hell, an old squaw can squat all day long scratching in the creek bottom."

"Oh, they have intestinal fortitude, Mitt, believe me. But they're not warriors, they're treasure seekers. They'll crater, but when? You promised they'd be out of there a month ago."

Hollis was under tremendous pressure to get that rich vein mined as soon as possible. And he had bigger problems than a bunch of mule-headed prospectors. The Sioux had recently succeeded in driving out a U.S. Army geological team sent into the Black Hills to explore the actual extent of gold deposits. And the massacre of a white settlement east of here, led by the fearsome renegade Inkpaduta, had gone unpunished by an American army now embroiled in the Mormon War. So now the Sioux felt understandably emboldened. Blackburn had to clear up these local troubles and get that color out of the ground damn soon before the savages organized in force.

"Well, it won't be long now," Brennan insisted, fingering the heavy brass studding of his belt. "There's enough of 'em sick that they've built a pesthouse. And if no doctors or medicine get in there, plenty will go under."

"Perhaps," Blackburn conceded. "But I have an uneasy feeling since Orrin and Boyd stupidly dumped those sick men to die instead of leaving them in Wyoming. I fear that mistake will come back to bite us. Especially if this Trailsman chap is given an opportunity to horn in. With his kind, either you strike first or you're sunk."

Those six men had all worked claims near the Alliance Mining Company's other major western operation, this one out in Wyoming. Blackburn had thus learned of the fever outbreak, by telegraphic dispatch, in plenty of time to send men out there to infect clothing and get it sneaked into a supply delivery from Rapid City to Busted Hump.

"We did strike first," Brennan assured him. "By now he's flat enough to slide under a door."

Blackburn started to reply, but a loud bell clanging from a nearby shaft house cut him off. He watched miners, with the unnaturally pale skin of men who work long hours underground, climb out of the skip that took them down to the stopes and back up. The new crew, wearing helmets with fat candles mounted in front, climbed into the skip. The hoist man hit a lever, steam escaped in a hissing sigh, the huge hoist wheels turned, and down they plunged into the dank bowels of the earth.

"Let's hope you're right this time," Blackburn told his lackey when it was quiet enough to speak again. "There are enough flies in the ointment as it is. I heard a preacher say once that 'Providence is operating on a grand scale to accomplish its designs.' And so am I, Mitt. So am I."

The moment that rocky slope began hurtling down to crush him, Fargo had to make a critical life-or-death decision—and he had perhaps the space of a heartbeat to make it.

He was almost exactly halfway across the rocky slope. Bolting straight for the far end might seem most logical. But a quick glance at the rock tonnage bounding down toward him showed that the largest mass of the slide seemed concentrated in that direction.

There was no time to dither. Making an instant decision, he yanked his horse around to reverse direction, boot heels hammering the Ovaro's flanks.

The first rocks and chunks of scree began flashing past man and horse. The stallion could absorb a few minor hits, and so could Fargo. But he also knew that any one of those chunks could smash a man's skull like an eggshell. A horse's brain was a much smaller target. He hooked his right leg around the saddle horn for an anchor, then slid most of his body to the left, putting his mount between himself and the blast debris. His right arm clung to the Ovaro's neck.

A gray-black cloud of dirt and pulverized rock choked man and beast. The plucky stallion laid back his ears and lengthened his stride, galloping blind now in the choking cloud.

A rock thudded off Fargo's saddle fender, another struck the Ovaro's shoulder and grazed Fargo's elbow in a fiery scrape. The roar sounded like a dozen trains about to pulverize them. The bulk of the debris was only seconds away now, and at any moment Fargo expected to either be smashed or bowled over that sheer cliff.

"Yiii—eeee—*yah!*" he shouted in the Ovaro's ear, and for good measure he gave the sensitive ear a quick, hard bite. He had found that sometimes, the best way to motivate a horse was to get him pissed off.

The outraged Ovaro lowered himself like a tight spring coiling, then gave a mighty leap just as the heaviest debris wiped out the trail behind them. That last, desperate effort had saved them. Miraculously, they had reached the safe part of the trail just in the nick of time.

Fargo, shaken, torqued himself back up into the saddle and eased back on the reins. A quick inspection revealed only a small cut on the Ovaro's right shoulder.

When the dust finally settled behind them, however, the damage was clear: The only high-altitude trail across Ragged Top Mountain was now a massive, impassable jumble.

That left only the canyon route—smack through land occupied by Alliance Mining.

"Our clover was deep that time, old war horse," he told the sweat-matted stallion.

But events had now taken an ominous turn. Fever victims were in desperate need of a doctor and medicine, yet he'd just lost valuable time. There was nothing for it now, Fargo decided, but to return to Busted Hump. He'd rest and graze the Ovaro while Elijah and Pow helped him plan a new, nighttime route past the Alliance Mining Company's hired killers.

One thing for sure: that was *not* a routine mining blast, but a calculated attempt to kill him.

The brothers were still waiting at their sentry post overlooking Busted Hump. When they spotted the dust-coated Fargo emerge from the thorny deadfall, leading his horse, they gawked as if he were Lazarus emerging from his tomb.

"We heard the explosion," Pow greeted him. "Tell you the straight, Mr. Fargo, we had you figured for a dead'un."

"Glad to see you still sassy," Elijah added.

"By the skin of my teeth," Fargo admitted. "My mistake was in expecting to be shot at. I wasn't looking for a mountain peak to be tossed on top me."

"That hell-begotten Hollis Blackburn is tricky as a redheaded woman," Pow assured him. "C'mon, Mr. Fargo, let's get you down to camp. Your horse needs tending, and you could use a quick bath in the creek. We appreciate the effort, though."

"The effort's far from over," Fargo assured them. "Me, I'm bullheaded. When I can't raise the bridge, then I just lower the river. Whoever it is can't be covering the entire Black Hills. I only need to get past their perimeter, and I'm heading out soon as it's full dark."

Fargo, leading the Ovaro by the bridle reins, fell into step single file behind Elijah and Pow. He followed them down a steep, narrow footpath descending into Spearfish Canyon and the prospector's camp of Busted Hump. Fargo saw, in his first glance around, that the rustic settlement ranged from prospectors with gravel pans, working elbow bends in the creek, to a few small mines with crude wooden headframes dotting the higher elevations.

Elijah sent him a cross-shoulder glance.

"Mister Fargo, my hand to God. When me and Pow first got here, you could take a reg'lar butcher knife and scratch gold outta the cracks in the rocks. These diggin's was *that* rich. Even now most of us get by with a pick, a shovel, a pan—and some sluice boxes we've knocked together."

Despite the fever outbreak and other problems besetting Busted Hump, Fargo saw life was still pretty much business as usual. Prospectors dotted Spearfish Creek and nearby erosion seams. A gangly kid carrying a water yoke, full pails dangling at either end, worked his way from claim to claim. Fargo spotted a few smaller children down near the creek, catching polliwogs in glass jars.

A closer look, however, suggested these folks were truly up against it.

Most of the clothes those kids were wearing had been sewn from old sacking or tent cloth. And many of the residents looked gaunt and hollow-eyed, sure signs of chronic hunger. Clearly they were being starved out by a ruthless foe—perhaps the same foe, Fargo realized, who almost freed my soul today.

Pow seemed to read some of Fargo's thoughts.

"Before Hollis Blackburn ordered all the poisoning," he said, "there was plenty of ducks and geese near the creek. Deer, rabbits, and quail in the thickets. We still flush some game, but it's way down."

He pointed toward a spot where a huge backwater had formed behind a wide bend in the creek. "Today some of that English bastard's two-legged cockroaches managed to tear out our brush dam upstream. Flooded damn near five acres of claims."

" 'Pears we took too long to starve out," Elijah tossed in. "So now he's going to do the job quick with plague and floods. You might say the man's biblical in his thinking."

Fargo noticed armed men at several approaches to the camp. "I see you've posted sentries," he said with approval.

"Me 'n Pow organized a twenty-four-hour guard even before Hollis Blackburn let loose his dogs on us."

Fargo said, "Sioux?"

Elijah nodded. "They've hit us a couple times, mostly to steal off horses and butcher meat. But they want us gone, too. Hell! On a good day I earn the same wages a cowhand makes in a month. My only mistake was giving in when Dotty insisted the family stay together."

"This ain't no place for women or kids," Fargo agreed.

"No, and I aim to get 'em out just as soon as it's safe to. I only hope it ain't too late."

They had reached the canyon floor. By now many of the residents had spotted the tall, bearded stranger leading a pinto stallion. Some of the faces were hostile. But Fargo never blamed folks for wariness toward strangers—especially armed strangers. Some men came west to escape injustice, others to escape justice. Folks had to be careful because it was not always easy to tell them apart.

However, one local, at least, was anything but hostile—a shapely little blond-haired muffin who was making come-hither eyes at Fargo from the doorway of a clapboard shack with a stick-and-mud chimney. She was barefoot and wore a calico skirt with a man's flannel shirt, amply swollen around her impressive breasts. While she watched Fargo like a cat on a rat, she pulled a horn comb through her loose, spun-gold tresses. Her lips were slightly puffy, as if swollen from passionate kissing.

"That tidy little bit of frippit coquetting with you right now," Pow informed him, "is named Mary Ellen Guidry. She's got two sisters, both so homely you could toss 'em in a pond and skim ugly for a month. But *she* sure 'nuff panned out high-grade, huh? Look at them honeydew melons."

"She's gotta have a man," Fargo pointed out. "Or else, in a woman-scarce place like this, you boys would be shooting each other to get her."

"Had her a man," Pow corrected him. "Several, matter fact. The last one got killed by Sioux 'bout three months ago when he wandered too far from these here diggin's looking for color. That's the trouble—he was rich, left her plenty of money if she just keeps occupying his claim until his brother gets here from Illinois to work it. Her being so rich, she's been colder than last night's mashed potatoes toward the rest of us prospectors, won't be nobody's reg'lar night woman. Seems to have an eye on you, though, Mr. Fargo."

That might be a pleasant interlude, Fargo told himself, meeting her sly, slanted gaze. But with all these horny stags in camp, he didn't want to sow resentment. Scratch a prospector and you'll find an iron-fisted brawler. . . .

"Hold on to your money belt," Elijah warned their visitor. "That's Philly Tyler ahead, our local 'doctor,' standing out front of his shack. If he can't hook you, he'll rook you."

Fargo spotted a muttonchopped, moon-faced man who looked like he'd just stepped out of a half-dimer with his fancy dude hat and embroidered bat-wing chaps. One of the many parasites drawn to goldstrike camps and tolerated because they livened up the place. This one, judging from the signs plastered on his shack, was a quack selling the new patent medicines and other guaranteed miracle cures.

"Try the latest sensation from Austria, my dusty friend!" he greeted Fargo. "Take the water cure! Wash and be healed! I am Hiram Tyler, Physician and Healer, of Philadelphia. Trained in the use of rinses, douses, and douches for spiritual and physical aches! Step into my miracle spa and be transformed! Only two dollars."

A toothy grin split Fargo's weathered face. "Douches? Every deck has its jokers, huh?"

"Ahh, of course, I should have seen it right off! Obviously, sir, you are a man who knows gee from haw. You're a Royal's man," Philly Tyler changed his spiel without missing a beat, instantly producing a bottle from a pocket of his bulging hopsack coat. "Royal's Hop Bitters, my bearded buckaroo. The invalid's friend and hope. Cures hangovers, lumbago, cancer, bilious complexion, bloating, cramps, childbed fever, whooping cough, stove-up joints, consumption, and the trots. One dollar takes it."

"That stuff's nothing but grain alcohol and sugar water," Fargo scoffed, starting to shoulder by. "Don't cure nothing. Just gets you so drunk you don't care."

"Lord love us, I see you have a mind like a steel trap, my intrepid bachelor of the saddle. But you also appear to be a betting man, am I right? I'll make you an ironclad offer right here in front of witnesses."

Philly pointed at Fargo's feet. "I'll tell you *exactly* where you got those boots. If I'm wrong, I'll pay you five dollars, one solid gold quarter-eagle. If I'm right, you pay me only four bits. Now, sir, you can't beat *that* offer with a stick."

Fargo knew he was being fleeced, but good-naturedly went along. "All right, I'll bite. Where?"

"You got them boots . . . *on your feet*," Philly announced triumphantly, holding out his hand.

Fargo laughed and paid up.

"I warned you," Elijah said as they moved on. His troubled gaze shifted toward the log pesthouse, where several new fever patients had just been quarantined. "Philly's good for a few grins, but he can't cure a boil. We don't get a real doc in here in a puffin' hurry, there's gonna be plenty of fresh graves."

They headed toward a fairly solid raw-lumber shack with hides tacked over the windows to keep the weather out. To one side, a few wolf skins were drying on stretchers. A slab door with leather hinges swung open and a towhead boy about twelve years old came outside.

"My son Jimmy," Elijah told Fargo. "Boy, take Mr. Fargo's horse for him. Rub him down good. Wash off that cut, then salve it. Fork him in a little hay, too."

Fargo had already spotted the nearby pole corral. It held only one sore-used horse, so thin its hip sockets stood out.

"Never mind that hay, Jimmy," Fargo said. "I grained him good earlier. Just make sure he gets water."

"Yessir!"

The kid eagerly grabbed the reins, but couldn't get the Ovaro to budge.

"Don't look right at a horse when you lead it, son," Fargo advised him. "Makes 'em skittish if they don't know you."

Elijah, Fargo, and Pow went inside. The interior was humble but clean: a deal table with an oilcloth, a cowhide trunk, dry goods boxes for chairs. Raw-plank bedsteads were covered with shuck mattresses. The legs of the beds were set in bowls of kerosene to keep the bedbugs off.

A woman in a faded muslin apron was pouring boiling water into a leach to make lye soap. Her once pretty face showed the strain of hard living and constant worrying. Fargo noticed that the baby on her hip wore a flour-sack diaper. Like its mother, the child seemed listless from hunger.

"My wife Dotty," Elijah said. "Dotty, Mr. Skye Fargo."

The gaze she turned toward him was one Fargo got often from women: a combination of attraction and a little mistrust. But she sent him a weary smile.

"I apologize for our home, Mr. Fargo," she greeted him. "This is only temporary."

"That apology is wasted on me, ma'am," he assured her. "Everything I own in the world is either on me or my horse."

"Dotty," Elijah said, "Mr. Fargo could use a lump of soap and a towel."

She finished her task, then handed him a yellowish lump of soap and a rough scrap of towel.

"There's a bathing pool in the creek, 'bout a hunnert yards north from here," Elijah told him. "You can't miss it—it's all hemmed in by willows so it's private."

"Watch out for Mary Ellen," Pow teased him as Fargo headed out. "Them was hungry eyes she turned on you. And once that gal gets a hunger, she generally has her a meal."

Dotty sniffed. "*That* one's second-hand, if you take my meaning?"

Fargo had enjoyed plenty of first-rate times with second-hand women. But he wisely held silent and headed back toward Spearfish Creek to wash off the trail dust. He found the natural bathing pool easily, a wide spot where the creek was well screened by willows.

He left his clothes in a heap on the grassy bank, his gun belt folded on top. As a precaution he slid the Arkansas Toothpick from its sheath and took it with him when he waded out into thigh-deep water and sat down in the cold but bracing creek.

He slid the knife under one foot to hold it and began working up a lather. Fargo plunged his sudsy head under to rinse it. When he surfaced again, he heard it: the snapping of a dry stick from the bank behind him.

Quick as a striking snake he whirled, right arm drawn back to toss the Arkansas Toothpick.

Mary Ellen Guidry stood watching him. When she spoke, her Southern accent flowed like sorghum poured warm.

"You goin' to kill me, mister, just for sneaking a little ol' peek atcha?"

Fargo grinned, flipping the knife point first into a nearby log. He glanced around, making sure no one else was near.

"If you're gonna watch me bathe, cupcake," he told her, "you might's well see something."

Fargo stood up, dripping wet. Her approving eyes traveled the long length of his muscle-corded body, then paused about in the middle.

"My lands! I'd like to see *that* when it's angry."

"Oh, he gets spittin' mad," Fargo assured her. "Care to provoke him?"

"I aim to, sugar," she replied, her voice husky with lust. "But not here. Philly Tyler saw me come this way, he's prob'ly selling tickets right now. You'll be staying the night?"

"Regrettably, just until dark."

"That's a few hours off still, we'll figure *some*thing out," she promised, taking one last, lingering look at his impressive manhood. "I hope you're as good with that as you are with the knife."

A moment later she was gone. A little smile flitted across Fargo's lips as he began sudsing his armpits.

This day had started with death, then progressed to a near-fatal rockslide. But chances looked good it was going to end much more pleasantly than it began.

<hr>

3

"Shove your feet under the table, Mr. Fargo," Elijah greeted the Trailsman when he returned from his bath. "It ain't high-grade eats, but it'll stay your belly."

The meal was indeed meager: a little watery bean soup and some crusts of corn bread. Fargo was hungry, but he would rather have left it all for the family. However, they were a proud bunch, and he was doing them a greater injury by refusing their humble hospitality.

"Actually, I wouldn't mind wrapping my teeth around some grub," he said, straddling a dry goods box and scooting it up to the table.

"Wish we had flour for biscuits," Powhatan remarked. "Dotty's biscuits're so light you gotta hold 'em down."

Pow had his own shelter, but being unmarried he took his meals with his brother and sister-in-law.

"We need pertection," he said bitterly. "Use to, a feller could run a buckboard through to Sturgis and back in two days, keep the camp supplied. Now all the soldiers're gone and we got Injins and white devils dealing us misery. It makes a man ireful! Them damn milk-livers in Congress don't care a jackstraw about us folks on the frontier."

"That's right. Which means a man out west can't be looking to others to protect him," Fargo pointed out. "So it's best to look close before you wade in. Prospecting ain't the problem, it's where you're doing it. There's bigger strikes on the Comstock—safer, too."

"Hell, you're right," Elijah admitted. "Me and Pow didn't choose this place, nor even this line of work, right off. We tried farming in Kansas, but grasshoppers ate us out. So we come west to try the fur trade. We done all right for a spell, but after the beaver trapped out, we stayed on out west to prospect. Oh, it's been a hell buster. Work goes on from can to can't. Ain't no other clocks. We measure out our toil in sweat."

"And there was a time," Pow pitched in, "before Hollis Blackburn set hisself up as God, when *all* of us around here had money to toss at the birds. Shoo! Maybe it's time to cut loose from these here diggin's. There's times I'd chuck all of it for a strip of good growing dirt and a solid cabin."

Fargo chewed, swallowed, then shook his head.

"Once a man mates with despair," he told Pow, "it's over. Like I said, personally, I wouldn't be here in the Black Hills poking for gold in the first place—not with women and kids along and the Sioux strong as they are, getting blood in their eyes. I hope you folks *do* pull stakes, when it's safe to do it and you're good and ready. But you *are* here right now, and this Hollis Blackburn ain't got no more rights to the gold than any of you. In fact, has Blackburn ever produced a legitimate deed for the Alliance Mining property he's already claiming?"

"Never showed us nothing," Elijah said. "Claims he's got a land warrant. Also claims some Pennsylvania senator is in on it with him, got them permission for—for—ah, hell, I forget the term—"

"Temporary domain," Dotty supplied.

"That, yeah. Means they don't own the land permanent like, but they can use it for a time."

24

"It's hogwash printed on pretty paper," Fargo insisted.

"Sure it is. And I don't crawfish to *nobody*," Elijah fumed. "Problem is, us prospectors ain't much as gunfighters. Oh, we got a few boys up from deep Texas, they can cut up rough if they have to. But most of us, hell, we're just sodbusters from east of the Mississippi. Blackburn, he's got frosty killers—men who'll plug you in the back, then ride off to lunch like it's none of their business."

"And even if his hired killers don't fire another shot," Pow added, "mountain fever may finish Blackburn's dirty work. We burnt up them infected duds, but the damage is already done."

"Three more cases of fever confirmed today," Dotty spoke up, her face drawn with deep worry lines. "Poor souls, they've been moved to the pesthouse. That's nineteen cases, so far. But how many more of us will catch it? Weak as folks in this camp are from hunger, them that's already sick, they'll last maybe three days, at the most, without medicine."

"That's why I'm heading out again soon as it's dark," Fargo assured her. He looked at Elijah. "But I'll need to somehow sneak past the area controlled by the Alliance Mine's guns. Then get back through with a doc and some supplies. Got a good route for me?"

"That one's got me treed," Elijah admitted. "Ain't no middle way—you'll have to take the canyon route now, right through their mining property. Leastways, if you want to get past that blast area on Ragged Top."

Fargo nodded. "Beard the lion in his own den, huh? Sometimes the plan that seems too reckless is the best choice. Give me the lay of the canyon."

"You'll strike out due south and follow the creek until you reach Roughlock Falls in about four, five miles. Take care from there on out. That's the boundary of the Alliance mining outfit. You won't be clear of their claim until you hit the Little Spearfish. You ignore the smaller creek, follow Spearfish due south, bearing gradually southeast. It's rough terrain. But you won't miss Thunderhead Mountain. It's always covered by dark clouds spittin' lightning bolts. Shoshone Falls sits just past it to the south."

Little Jimmy Stone had been listening while the men talked.

"Jimmy, I checked, and you took good care of my horse," Fargo told him. "Even cleaned up his cut. I appreciate that, son."

"What's your horse's name, Mr. Fargo?" the kid asked.

"I never name a horse, Jimmy. Generally, it's not the custom out here in the West."

"How's come?"

Dotty Stone, her youngest child on her knee, looked a warning at Fargo. But it was Elijah who spoke up.

"Because, too often out here, a man has to shoot his horse, boy, to end its suffering. That's how come."

"Oh. But don't—"

"Jimmy, shush up and eat your supper," his mother told him.

"Can't," he replied. "It hurts when I swallow. And I don't feel so good."

Fargo watched Elijah and Dotty exchange a panicked glance. Difficulty swallowing was an early symptom of mountain fever. Dotty reached across the table to feel Jimmy's forehead.

"Son, you best go lie down," she said gently. "I'll bring you some honey and tea directly."

When the boy was out of earshot, Dotty looked at Elijah. "He's burning up," she said, a tear sneaking past her attempt at a brave face.

Pow looked like he wanted to kick something. Elijah just looked numb and slowly nodded. He was a strong, big-fisted man, but disease was one enemy he couldn't beat into submission.

"We'll know in a few more hours if he has to go into the pesthouse," was all he said.

Fargo glanced at the sun on the floor and saw it was getting late. He stood up. "This scrape ain't over yet, folks. Remember that. But if I'm riding tonight, I'd best rest up until dark. Got some place where I can spread my blanket?"

The brothers took him outside and pointed to a raw-lumber structure with a crooked stovepipe chimney. It was about fifty yards downslope, closer to Spearfish Creek.

"If you don't mind sleeping in a dead man's bed," Pow explained, "that shack ain't been claimed. Belonged to Frank Winkler. He only prospected mornings, spent the rest of his time running traplines. We warned him he was wandering too far from camp. Found him shot to rag tatters. Whoever done it rode shod horses, so it wasn't Injins. Besides, they wouldn't waste lead like that. A Sioux would just as soon kill a white man with a rock, save the bullet for game.

"The bed ain't much," Pow added. "Just some leather webbing strung 'twixt two walls."

"Mr. Fargo," Elijah spoke up, finally recovering from the shock of Jimmy's sickness, "I ain't tryin' to poke too close along your backtrail. But why are you taking this risk for us?"

Fargo shrugged. "When folks are in trouble, a man gives them a hand. Besides, it's more in my line of work than yours."

Elijah glanced back into his shack. "See, about Jimmy . . . me and Dotty, we've already buried three children. Him and little Sarah are all we got left, the poor little sprouts. You might think the buryin' gets easier, Mr. Fargo, but it don't. Not when it's your own kids. I thank you kindly for your help. We all do."

"I'll give it my best," he promised. "Meantime, keep your sentries posted. Don't let the fever outbreak destroy your camp discipline. That's when your enemies will strike."

Elijah pressed a heavy doeskin pouch into Fargo's hand. "All nuggets, pure gold. Supplies will run dear, and I hear that doc's a cantankerous old drunkard. He'll likely need persuading before he agrees to ride clear through the entire Black Hills."

As he headed toward the shack, lugging his tack and gear, Fargo cast a hopeful eye toward Mary Ellen Guidry's doorway. However, he was immediately accosted by Philly Tyler's booming circus bark.

"Ah, it's our untutored son of the sagebrush! What you require, sir, is a genuine Sioux Indian scalp. This hirsute masterpiece you're looking at right now was lifted from the Sioux war chief Medicine Flute. I won it in a poker game, up at Fort Union, from the very soldier who took it in the heat of battle."

Fargo grinned after one glance at the "scalp" in Philly's hand.

"Philly, you can lay a feather on a rock and call it a sofa, too, but *I* ain't sleeping on it. And I ain't buying that horse-hair scalp. Hell, you clipped it from *my* horse's tail. You're lucky he didn't kick you halfway to the moon."

Philly sighed tragically, quickly shoving the horse hair back into a coat pocket. "Friend, there's the problem with you rugged frontier types—plenty of guts but no imagination. But I *know* you simple rustics like flashy entertainment. Watch this."

Philly produced a silver dollar and deftly walked it back and forth across the knuckles of his left hand.

"How's that for a show?" he demanded. "I can juggle, perform sleight of hand, and dazzling feats of legerdemain that have awed royal courts everywhere on the European continent."

"That right? I guess them kings and queens are easy to please."

He started to walk past, but Philly called out: "Check your holster, Mr. Fargo."

Fargo did. His Colt was missing. Grinning like a Cheshire cat, Philly handed it back to him. This time, when he spoke, Philly dropped the showman's act.

"The whole secret to trickery is *diversion*, Mr. Fargo. While you were watching my left hand, my right stole your gun. The whole camp knows by now what you're trying to do for us. I think you need to keep that principle of diversion in mind as you try and figure a way to slip past Hollis Blackburn's thugs."

Fargo was beginning to understand that quack and con man Philly Tyler was something more than just an opportunistic parasite. But whose colors was he flying, if any?

"If you got an idea," Fargo replied, "toss it into the hotchpot."

"Just a moment."

Philly stepped inside his sign-plastered "spa" and emerged a moment later, handing Fargo a can of blasting powder.

"I think one good explosion deserves another, Mr. Fargo. There's a powder shack that sits on the northern edge of the Alliance Mine site. Clearly marked. If that shack was to go up? Why, it'd light up the Dakota Territory. More to the point, every thug they've got in the area would come running back like bees to see the damaged hive. A careful man could slip by in all the confusion."

Fargo grinned, eyeing the city dude closely. "How much for the powder?"

"Gratis, my bearded caballero."

"Just out of the goodness of your heart?" Fargo said, watching closely. "Is that it?"

"Of course not, it's pure self-interest. Oh, I don't get rich here in Busted Hump, no. I've raked in more money in end-of-track towns and even buffalo camps. But these folks don't shoot at me when they get snockered. Plus, I like these prospectors. They work hard and leave the land mostly as they found it. Hollis Blackburn and his ilk destroy mountains and reroute rivers—and live high on the hog off other men's suffering and labor. On top of all that, they're cold-blooded killers."

Philly shrugged his shoulders. "Me? Sure, I'd steal a hot stove and come back for the smoke. But Philly Tyler never hurt another human being's person. And scum who deliberately spread deadly diseases deserve to face justice. You, Mr. Fargo, strike me as a man used to dispensing justice. Good day, sir, and confusion to our enemies."

Fargo walked on down to the shack, still trying to decide just whose side Philly was really backing. He pulled the hide off the only window to air the place out a little. Then he spread his blanket on the leather-web bed, draped his gun belt over a wall nail, and kicked off his boots.

Fargo had learned to fall asleep fast and roll out on time. Nor were erotic dreams unusual for a man who spent much time on the trail. But this one he started having now was getting much better than most of the dreams, much more exciting and real. Mary Ellen Guidry's passion-puffed lips were wrapped around his manhood, her frenzied tongue swirling all over the tip, her bottom teeth raking his shaft just hard enough to hurt so nice. . . .

So nice . . . .

"So nice!" a woman's lust-husky voice moaned, and Fargo's eyes snapped open.

Enough daylight still streamed through the window to show a wild confusion of blond hair fanned out over his belly. His buckskin trousers had been opened, and Mary Ellen Guidry was licking a long, delicious line up and down the length of his rigid shaft.

"Either I'm moon-crazy," she greeted him, "or it's *you*, Skye Fargo, that's got me all shuddery and slippery 'tween my legs."

She took him in her mouth again, tasting him with greedy slurps. The Trailsman groaned encouragement.

"I see *this* girl's feeling sparky."

"It's your fault," she pouted, licking his sac now. "Teasing me like you done down at the bathing pool. 'Course, you wouldn't be the first man who talked big and then couldn't cut the bacon in bed."

"Honey, I'll not only cut it, I'll cure it, then cook it so hot it sizzles."

"Lord, you *do* make a gal's face flush, talking like that. I'm terrible glad you ain't left yet. I figure about an hour still before dark. Can you stay in the saddle that long?"

"Depends on the filly," he told her. "Let me have a better look at what I'll be riding."

Mary Ellen had already shucked out of her dress and now only an embroidered chemise of thin muslin covered her.

"I know it sounds prideful," she told him as she started to pull it up over her head. "But I could have any man in this camp. 'Course, most of these old boys around here stink bad and got no women to choose from. They don't never even ask a single gal her age—all they require is teeth."

The chemise came off, baring a solid, curvaceous body with a pair of hefty, plum-capped nipples.

"This is my hope chest," she informed him, moving in so close he could feel her animal heat. "*Hope* you like it?"

"Honey," he assured her, eagerly kneading her breasts and tweaking her pliant nipples stiff, "you could have any man *any*where. You're a nice little package."

"Oh, mud-grubbing prospectors are all right, I reckon, for them gals as ain't partic'lar. Me, I cotton to man flesh what's a little different. More dangerous and exciting . . . *m-m-m*, yeah, just like that, that's ni-i-ce!"

Fargo had stopped her foolish chatter by popping one of

her chewy gumdrop nipples into his mouth to suck and tease it. This had the effect, on her, of tossing a lit match into a gas pocket.

"Oh, Skye, you do that *so* nice! Lookit what you're doin' to me."

Boldly she guided one of his hands to the wet, warm nest between her legs. She was copiously flowing. "Wanna pet my puppy?"

Her tone was hungry, pleading, and fired Fargo's lust even hotter. He expertly coaxed her innermost lips open, sliding a finger inside her hot slipperiness. She gasped, her whole body visibly trembling.

"I been needing a real man inside me for a long time," she groaned as she climbed onto the bed and straddled him. "And judging from the size on you, you randy stallion, it'll be a cold day in hell 'fore I find a better one."

Her trembling hand gripped him and bent him to the perfect angle. She nudged him just into the moist portal, gripping and squeezing only the tip. Then, with a fast twitch of her shapely hips, she took about half of him into her hot, wet depths, gasping with delight as he opened her up.

"Good God a-gorry!" she cried out, shivering and sighing. "Oh, Skye, you're just filling me up inside!"

She plunged down the rest of the way, and Fargo felt his manhood parting the deepest walls of her love tunnel. Hot, luscious, tickling pleasure washed over him as she suddenly turned into a tiger in a whirlwind, riding him like he was a bucking bronco.

"Long time!" she gasped.

"Since you had it?"

"No, *do* me a long, long time—oh, oh, like—like *that!*"

A series of climaxes washed over her, only making her more greedy. Up and down she pistoned, faster, harder, taking his curving length from base to tip, firing an insistent heat and pressure in his groin. But Fargo summoned all his will power and held off, letting this horny gal get the "long time" she obviously needed.

However, instead of gradually spending her passion, she only seemed to go even crazier after each explosive string of climaxes. It was as if she were a fire, and his thrusts were the fuel feeding it. Soon she was bouncing up and down even more forcefully, uttering incoherent gasps and moans as she drove both of them toward a powerful final release.

"NOW, Skye!" she finally cried out.

His entire body arced like a bow as he groaned in powerful release. This drove Mary Ellen over the edge, and she started slamming into him so hard Fargo felt the suspended bed begin to pull loose from the walls.

"Honey," he warned, "we're—"

But it was too late. With a final banshee scream of delight, Mary Ellen plunged down to impale herself on him. Not only did the bed tear loose, but it brought down both walls it was attached to! The shack caved in on them with a crash of collapsing boards.

Mary Ellen screamed, Fargo cursed, as lumber buried them. The commotion disturbed the entire camp. Everywhere dogs started barking, and Fargo could hear people running from every direction to see what was wrong.

"You all right?" he asked her, tossing boards aside.

"Lord have mercy! I knew you'd be good, Skye Fargo. But that's the very first time any man ever brought the house down around me!"

By now daylight was fading. But enough light remained for everyone to see the naked woman scrambling to cover herself.

"Hey, Skye!" a voice he recognized as Pow's sang out. "Did you at least get to the finish line before the twister hit?"

More men were calling out jokes. Fargo, who had already lost about eight hours since beginning his journey to Thunderhead Mountain and Shoshone Falls, figured this was a damn good time to light out.

He knocked boards aside and grabbed his tack, gear, and weapons. He gave Mary Ellen a quick peck. "Thanks, dumplin'. Nicest dream I ever woke up to."

"Wait, Skye! I know where you're going, and you're just sticking your head in a noose! Stay and play with me? I got money. Skye! Come *back* here, damn you, I want more!"

But Fargo, sticking to the shadows in his embarrassment, headed quickly up toward the pole corral, carrying his boots. He quickly tacked the Ovaro, then wrapped his blanket inside his slicker and secured the roll with his cantle straps. When the stallion was rigged, he lifted the stirrup flap for a final check of the cinch.

Usually, Fargo avoided night riding in unfamiliar terrain. But as he swung aboard and reined the Ovaro around, he reminded himself there was no other choice.

As he rode out, a rising moon lighted the very tips of the surrounding mountains like silver patina. But Fargo saw another image, one of six dead prospectors with rocks piled over their bodies. Just as rocks had nearly buried *him* alive a few hours earlier. He now had less than three days to get a doctor and medicine to Busted Hump—and time was the least of his enemies.

He could feel the cool weight of the can of blasting powder tucked inside his shirt, and hear Philly Tyler's words all over again: *One good explosion deserves another.*

The three of them met in a big equipment shed owned by the Alliance Mining Company: Mine Captain Mitt Brennan, Caswell "Cas" Merrill, and Orrin Jones. Boyd Lofley was supposed to be there, too, but as usual he was late.

"Boys," Mitt told them, "I'll give it to you with the bark still on it. We ain't working for just three hots 'n a cot now. We ain't never seen gravy like this. But after this latest foul-up today, Hollis is going to be screaming blue murder. *How* could you mutton heads have failed to douse that stranger's light? Hell, you used a keg of black powder! That whole ridge is rubble now."

The light was fading to grainy twilight in the shed's only window. Brennan lifted the glass chimney of a coal-oil lamp and turned up the wick. Then he thumb-scratched a lucifer and set it ablaze. The light flared up, making the men's shadows long and thin on the raw-lumber walls. This half of the equipment-jammed shed had been converted into Brennan's living quarters.

The door swung open, admitting a doltish-looking, slope-shouldered man wearing a black slouch hat and faded, filthy corduroy pants. They were tucked into boots sporting fancy Mexican spurs of pure silver, with savage four-inch rowels. He carried a percussion-action Sharps and wore a five-shot Colt in a chamois armpit holster.

"Where you been?" Brennan demanded. "Bust your leg in a badger hole?"

As usual Boyd Lofley ignored him, spurs chinging as he came farther into the room. Brennan tolerated the man's insolence because there was nothing too repugnant for Boyd's stomach. He'd kill children, old ladies, anyone he was ordered to kill. Such men were useful in this present business.

"Hand me that cheerwater," the new arrival told Orrin Jones, who was nursing a bottle of cheap wagon-yard whiskey.

Jones, a former hider, wore Apache-style knee-length moccasins and a campaign hat with the yellow cavalry cord. The buckskin sheath propped against his chair contained a .40 caliber New Haven Arms repeating rifle with a 20-shot magazine.

"You damn piker," Jones flung at Lofley as he handed him the liquor. "Why'n't *you* buy a bottle sometime?"

"And why don't *you* kiss my lily-white ass?"

"Never mind your damned bickering!" Brennan snapped, slacking into a horsehair-stuffed chair. "Hollis knows this stranger must have discovered those prospectors—who else would've bothered covering their bodies with rocks? Who's to say they were all dead when he found them? Now you idiots have bollixed up the explosion. Hollis ain't paying us the big money so we can ruin this operation. He expects a good day's work for a good day's pay."

Cas Merrill snorted. He stood hip-cocked against a wall, a blunt and bull-necked man wearing a flat-crowned hat and an eight-shot Smith & Wesson repeating pistol. A furrowed knife scar marred his right cheek.

"Hollis Blackburn's a sissy Limey," he sneered. "Soft-handed and dandified. Talks like a book."

"So what?" Mitt shot back. "He's got a good think piece on him and a pair of iron balls."

"Maybe. But there's something about that British bastard that just won't tally. I don't trust him."

Jones grinned as he grabbed the liquor back from Lofley. "Trust everybody, Cas—but always cut the cards."

Despite the waning light, the camp outside was a noisy and lively place. Men who were off shift loitered everywhere, drinking beer and pitching horseshoes, arm wrestling, betting on foot races—anything to alleviate the boredom of a mining camp.

"You don't *have* to trust Hollis," Mitt reminded all three men. "He pays good money, cash on the barrelhead."

Orrin, Cas, and Boyd had worked as a team for years now. Mitt, who once rode with them before meeting Hollis, had sent for the trio up in Wyoming's South Pass country, where they had survived by preying on migrating settlers.

"What I don't get," Cas complained, "is why Hollis keeps pussyfootin' around this thing? We got a free hand to handle it any way we want. Ain't nobody back in Washington City cares about a passel of fool prospectors out here in Zeb Pike's wasteland."

"Damn straight," Boyd took up the argument. "Why not just end it with one good strike? Us four plus we enlist some of the miners that are passable shots and just slaughter the whole shivaree. Hell, we can scatter around some clay pipes and other stuff, make it look like an Indian-led massacre."

"That's the gait," Cas said. "Ain't no blue-bellies around anyhow. And no sane lawman rides into the Black Hills. Best time to get 'er done is now, before any law noses in."

Mitt shook his head as if they were soft-brained children. "What's *best*, you pack of numskulls, is to avoid drawing law into it at all. Hollis is worried word of an outright massacre will put snow in the boots of his partner in Congress. But, see, disease wiping out a place, hell, that's just God's wrath. Now the whole plan is threatened because you didn't kill this newcomer on the pinto stallion. He was seen in Busted Hump *after* the explosion. If he gets through to a doc—"

"Ain't *no*body getting through to no doctor," Boyd cut in. He was in the habit of constantly snapping the wheel of a spur with his finger. He flicked at it now, irking the others, as he added: "Not in time to help those sourdoughs, anyhow."

"Can't be done," Orrin Jones agreed. "We got damn near a dozen renegades and half-breeds watching both the high country and canyon trails. Since the canyon trail is better hidden, we got it riddled with pitfall traps. Unless that stranger can grow wings and fly, he's a gone beaver."

"I still say," Cas grumped, "let's just put at the camp, get it over with. Make 'em fight or show yellow. To hell with this mountain fever and tearing out dams. Let's just put paid to it."

"Just keep following orders," Brennan said, his tone brooking no defiance. "Hollis pays the piper, so *he* calls the tunes. You three got one big job right now—making damn good and sure nobody gets through for help. And that includes making sure that help don't get in. Now get out there and earn your wages."

4

While a butter-colored full moon crept toward her zenith, Skye Fargo rode south following the lazy meanders of Spearfish Creek.

From the well-forested floor of Spearfish Canyon he could see mile-high hills towering all around him, cutting dark silhouettes against the blue-black night. A million stars shimmered in the bottomless sky, and the evening was mostly silent except for the pulsating chorus of insects and the occasional, irritated snorting of the Ovaro. The latest hatch of flies were thriving in the marshy backwaters of the creek and dealing the stallion misery.

For the first few miles Fargo followed a clearly marked trail that had probably begun as an ancient game trace. The night was well illuminated and time pressed, but Fargo refused to push the Ovaro beyond an easy trot. For one thing, he knew that night travel, especially in new terrain, was risky for any horse—and its rider if the horse came up lame. For another, he suspected more ambushers lay in wait. And they wouldn't be Sioux—not after dark, a time when few Plains Indians ventured far from camp.

Now and then he drew rein, halting to listen. And several times he dismounted to look for sign in the generous moon-wash. Each time he found plenty of animal tracks, and that fact comforted him. If the smell of humans was strong in an area, it would have driven off the wild animals.

Eventually, however, he came across recent tracks made

by an unshod pony. *Ponies*, Fargo corrected himself as he squatted on his heels and carefully studied the tracks. As Indians often did, these braves had ridden single file to make it harder for any trackers to count them. He was safe for now, after dark. But Fargo was almost certain this band were camped in these hills, watching everyone.

Nearby, a squirrel suddenly chattered a warning. Fargo wondered, as he stepped up into leather again, if *he* had disturbed it. Or had it been someone else?

He kneed the Ovaro into motion. The stallion broke into a trot, and now and then, to his right, Fargo glimpsed moonlight shimmering on the wide creek before dense juniper and pine thickets cut it from view again.

Despite his hair-trigger vigilance, he still felt the pleasant groin ache of his literal tumble with Mary Ellen. The memory of that shack caving in on them coaxed his lips into a smile.

Thus pleasantly distracted, Fargo had scant time to react when he rode smack into the ingenious trap. But everything seemed to happen in slowed-down nightmare time.

He had encountered this "trip-and-pit" set-up before. A large pitfall had been dug right across the trail, well disguised with brush and leaves. But a pitfall, by itself, often trapped the horse while forward momentum threw the rider clear. So whoever dug this pitfall had included a trip rope, tied low across the trail a couple of yards before the trap. The Ovaro went down hard, hurling Fargo straight over the saddle horn and into the pitfall.

The Ovaro almost tumbled in on top of his master, crushing him, but barely avoided it with a powerful twist that threw the stallion to one side of the trap, safe from falling. Fargo's feet crashed through the camouflaged cover, and he immediately spotted the sharpened wooden stakes, their poisoned tips glistening black in the moonlight. Only a fraction of an inch separated him from death by impalement, leaving Fargo to make a desperate, reckless bid to cheat the Reaper.

He managed to brace his feet against one dirt wall of the pit and push off hard, just barely clearing the poisoned spears. But the move left him off balance with no time to brace for impact before he slammed hard, head and left shoulder first, into the dirt just behind the stakes.

He felt a mule-kick impact, saw a bright orange starburst inside his skull, and Skye Fargo's world shut down to silence and darkness.

"It's mountain fever, all right, Elijah."

Dotty Stone's chilling words slid down her husband's spine like shards of ice. He stood in the moonlight outside his shack, smoking a clay pipe and saying a silent prayer for Jimmy, when Dotty came out with the gut-wrenching news.

"You're sure?" he pressed her.

She nodded, her eyes bright with unshed tears. "He's so hot you can't hardly touch him. And his throat glands are all puffed out. The poor child is getting delirious, doesn't even know what I'm saying to him."

"And little Sarah?"

"She's fine so far, thank the Lord. She's sound asleep."

Elijah nodded as he knocked the dottle out of his pipe by tapping it against his boot heel.

"All right then," he said wearily. "In a few hours Jimmy will be contagious. I'd best carry him on down to the pesthouse."

The quarantine building was being manned by Stacey Hanson and Reno Morgan, two immune volunteers who had survived mountain fever in the past.

Dotty fell into step beside her husband as he carried the semi-conscious boy down the canyon slope toward the pesthouse.

"Honest to John, honey," the big prospector said, his voice almost breaking, "I'm sorry I brought you and the kids with me this time. The *hell* was I thinking?"

"My fault too. I badgered you, I cried and pouted—"

"It's *my* fault," Elijah insisted, his voice heavy with self-loathing. "Either a man bends with the breeze or he breaks. Me and Pow was soft-brained fools to ever prospect in the Black Hills."

"Don't fret, Elijah," she tried to console him. "Maybe Mr. Fargo will bring help in time."

"Maybe he will, at that. He's a plumb good sort, and he'll sure's hell try. But I think it might be easier to hold the ocean back with a broom. God*damn* that bastard Hollis Blackburn!"

"Elijah, language like that won't favor the Creator toward us," Dotty scolded mildly.

But Elijah, a man slow to rile, was worked up now. His mouth twisted in anger under the shaggy mustache.

"If our boy dies, Dotty, I swear I'll kill Blackburn or die trying. God strike me down if I don't!"

The couple placed Jimmy on a cot outside the pesthouse and called to Stacey and Reno to come get him. On the way back to their shack, Elijah spotted a figure lurking in the shadows near the creek. He recognized the outline of the dude hat.

"That you, Philly?" he called out.

" 'Tis I, Elijah," the grifter replied.

"Something the matter?"

After a pause, Philly replied: "Oh, something usually is. But you might say that right now I'm waiting for a fireworks show to begin."

For uncounted minutes Fargo floated somewhere beneath the surface of awareness. Even before his eyes snapped open, he felt pain spiking into his head, left shoulder, and neck, so much pain it felt like a herd of buffalo had stampeded over his upper body.

But something else began to poke at awareness: the noise that had woken him up. A familiar, insistent buzzing sound, so close he even felt the vibration of the rattles.

The rattles!

When his eyes snapped open, he felt his heart leap into his throat. The coiled snake was so close to his face that, even in the moonlight, he could count the green speckles on its back.

Fargo knew the rattler's flicking tongue had already captured his odor particles. Now the sensitive touch receptors on its belly were poised to detect the slightest movement from this potential prey. Fargo knew that if he even twitched a finger, the rattler would bury its fangs in his face or neck—injecting the deadly venom close to his brain.

He willed himself to play dead, barely breathing while the agitated rattler calmed down somewhat. After several minutes the snake slithered away a few feet, and Fargo went instantly into action.

He could still feel the weight of his Colt in its holster. But the sound of a gunshot would carry far at night and alert his enemies. So Fargo slid the Arkansas Toothpick from his boot as he sprang up, trapping the snake's head under one heel.

Even after he sliced the reptile in two, the severed, headless part continued to thrash around. Fargo was careful to grind the head far down into the soft dirt. Though nerve dead, a snake could still inject its venom from pure reflex.

He whistled, and the well-trained Ovaro nickered in response, peering down into the pit. Each movement fired an excruciating ache in Fargo's sprained shoulder. But he had to take the pain as he began digging hand and footholds, climbing slowly and laboriously up out of the pitfall.

He was just dragging himself over the lip of the trap when Fargo heard it: the clinking of bit chains. More than one rider was approaching.

Wincing at the explosive pain in his injured shoulder, he vaulted into the saddle and tugged the rein hard left, veering into the dense wall of trees.

"Cas and Boyd are checking the pitfalls now," Mitt Brennan told his boss. "I sent Orrin to palaver with them renegades and half-breeds we've got scattered across—"

"Once again, Mitt, you're chewing it too fine," Hollis Blackburn cut in, though patiently. "I don't require the entire menu from soup to nuts. Remember, it's knowing too many *details* that sinks a man on the witness stand. I didn't send for you because I want up-to-the-minute briefing. I must warn you in the most forceful terms: This Skye Fargo is hell unleashed. By now he *should* have been . . . disposed of once and for all."

Hollis used a bootjack to pry off his tight boots, then propped his stockinged feet on a needlework footstool. A brick furnace had been constructed just to bake enough bricks to build this solid, comfortable house that he shared with Suzette, his French mistress. The stair railing of antique brass had been hauled in from St. Louis. Fancy lithographs on the walls depicted scenes of London. As the two men spoke in Blackburn's den, Suzette was playing a Chopin waltz on the elegant brass-inlaid rosewood piano in the parlor.

"We'll toss the net around that son of a bitch," Brennan vowed. "But the thing of it is, this Fargo knows 'b' from a banjo when it comes to survival. He's got 'hard twist' writ all over him."

Hollis, who was savoring snuff in his upper lip, sneered. "Would you like some cheese to go with that whine?"

Brennan's pox-scarred face looked confused. "Come again?"

"Never mind, just a bad pun. No excuses, Mitt—our mysterious buttinsky in buckskins *must* be . . . dealt with once and for all. Point taken?"

Mitt nodded.

"In the unlikely event that he does reach Shoshone Falls," Hollis remarked, "Coyote will be waiting to welcome him."

"I'd rather have Satan welcome me to hell," Mitt said with obvious conviction.

Hollis nodded, a smile flitting across his lips. "Indeed. At least the devil is willing to bargain."

He picked up a Belgian-made pinfire revolver from the table beside his chair. He rolled the cylinder against his palm to check the action.

"Now, as to the other matter we need to discuss," he resumed. "Ideally, Mitt, the cat simply sits by the gopher hole and bides its time. But thanks to the growing threat from the Sioux, *time* has become our worst enemy. I'm willing to wait a few more days, see if this . . . unfortunate fever outbreak finally drives the prospectors out of Busted Hump. If not? Well, the Lord helps those who help themselves."

Mitt, his hat balanced on one knee, sat forward in his chair. "Do you mean . . . a massed strike?"

"The whole kit and caboodle, as you Yanks say. Of course, *I* am issuing no such specific order. This conversation is simply theoretical. But certainly you've noticed something, Mitt. In the American West, you're just a face with a name. Nobody cares about your history. Unfortunately, nobody much cares about your future, either. In fact, on the frontier few things are cheaper than a man's life."

Brennan said, "I thought you were worried about word of a massacre leaking out?"

Hollis sighted down the filigreed barrel of the revolver, aiming it out a window at a nearby pile of ore tailings.

"I am. But a *fool*," he replied smugly, "may be defined as anyone who lets moral considerations hinder profits. Let me worry about the ultimate fate of Busted Hump. I want you and your men to concentrate on one task now: removing a human thorn named Skye Fargo."

5

Whoever his mystery visitors were, Fargo barely eluded them in time. He swerved off the canyon trail and took refuge in the maze of towering pine trees that grew everywhere throughout the Black Hills.

His trained ears counted two riders, and the sound of hoofs stopped somewhere near the pitfall. Since night was no time for most law-abiding folks to be traipsing around in rough country like this, Fargo suspected it was Alliance thugs checking their traps for human quarry. Which, if true, meant they were now alerted that he was on his way for help.

One thing was certain: if they had dug one pitfall, they had probably dug others elsewhere on the trail. So Fargo reluctantly decided to keep the creek in sight but remain among the trees.

The going wasn't so slow and rough as he'd expected it to be. Despite the density of the trees, they were mostly clear of lower branches. The combination of the Ovaro's excellent night vision and a full moon allowed Fargo to make reasonably good time.

He reached Roughlock Falls, at the juncture of Spearfish and Little Spearfish Creek. Now he knew he was on posted property claimed by the Alliance. Soon he had taken cover on a wooded ridge overlooking the entire mine complex, which was laid out below him in the moonlight like a painting.

Fargo studied it, making a mental map. A huge, man-made mountain of ore tailings told him where the mucking operation was set up. Several narrow shaft houses showed him where the skips—the steam lifts that transported miners above and below ground—were located. They were spaced widely apart and suggested this was a large-scale mining operation.

He noted long, low bunkhouses, various equipment sheds, and an assay shack. There was also a large brick house, an unheard-of luxury in these parts, on a knoll above the site.

The structure that most interested him, however, was a windowless building of slab lumber. It stood well off to one side, and the door was chained and padlocked. Any doubt that it contained explosives vanished when Fargo spotted the sentry seated out in front of it on a three-legged stool. He wore a hog leg .44 whose muzzle almost touched the ground. Other armed sentries prowled the perimeter of the camp.

"You're on your own for now, old trooper," he told the Ovaro.

He dropped the bridle and put the stallion on a long tether so he could drink from the creek and graze. Fearing it would just be in his way, Fargo left his Henry in its saddle boot. If he got his tail in a crack, he'd have to rely on his Colt and quick wits. With the can of blasting powder still tucked behind his shirt, he started down toward the mining camp, leapfrogging from tree to tree.

Soon, however, the trees thinned out and open hardpack took over. But Fargo now had another complication. The surrounding peaks had arrested some rain clouds, and one of the area's frequent and dramatic lightning shows had erupted. Brilliant flashes of bone white lightning turned night into day and placed Fargo at greater risk of discovery.

He tried to time the lightning flashes as he moved ever closer to that sentry in front of the explosives shack. Fargo's left shoulder felt a little better but still sent off quick stabs of pain. He was close enough now that he could hear the steady *chug-a-thump* of the big steam pumps used to keep water levels low in the stopes—the hollowed-out rooms, along the vein, where ore was dug out.

Keeping to the shadows when possible, he hooked around to one side of the shack. Fargo was barely out of sight when a man, carrying a pail and a bunch of metal cups on a string, joined the sentry.

"Patrick, you on'ry summagun, how's by you?" the new arrival greeted the sentry.

"Ah, sure and this job beats being back down in the stopes," Patrick replied in a thick Irish brogue. "But it does get boresome of a night."

The second man dipped a cup into the pail and handed it to the sentry. Fargo smelled coffee and suddenly wished he had a cup himself.

" 'Bout damn time you showed up," Patrick added. "Where the hell you been, Hank? Makin' whoopee with that walleyed squaw who does laundry?"

"She's better than that smelly old sheep *you* sleep with, you Cork County reprobate," Hank roweled him back.

Patrick raised his right hand as if swearing an oath. "Honest to Christ, Constable, I was only helping that sheep over the fence!"

Both men laughed, and Fargo silently joined in, telling himself he had to remember that joke.

Patrick took a sip of coffee and quickly spit it out. "God's trousers! You could cut a plug off that brew, boyo!"

"Damn straight. Coffee ain't ready until it'll float a horseshoe. See you again around midnight, you old blowhard."

Hank moved on to the next sentry post. Fargo slipped quickly around the front corner of the shack and tapped Patrick on the shoulder.

"Wha—? Mister, for the love of Mike, who are—?"

Patrick realized this was trouble and dropped his cup. He started to stand up, slapping for his big sidearm. Fargo, set solidly on his heels, sent a looping blow toward the guard's jaw. He found the knockout nerve, his punch landing so squarely it instantly unhinged the sentry's knees.

Fargo had nothing against any of these rank-and-file miners. Most were powerless, overworked, underpaid men at the mercy of bosses who treated them like disposable equipment. So he grabbed the unconscious man under the arms and dragged him well behind the shack, out of the potential blast area. Then he quickly gagged him with his own neckerchief and tied his ankles and wrists with rawhide thongs.

"Sorry, Paddy," he muttered. "But I got a diversion to create and you were blocking my trail."

That remark set Fargo to thinking, as he sneaked back to the explosives shack, about Philly Tyler and his motives. What if Philly had set him up? He could be in cahoots with Hollis Blackburn, and this blasting powder could have been deliberately dampened on the inside so it would do nothing but fizzle harmlessly when lit. The hope, perhaps, being that Fargo would be killed or captured in the attempt to use it.

The shack door was securely chained and locked, but a small crawl-space had been left under the floor to protect the powder charges from ground flooding. With many grunts and a lot of hip wiggling, Fargo worked half his body under the building.

He unscrewed the lid of the powder can, then shook out a thin fuse line of black powder. He set the can on its side, wriggled back out from under the shack, and took a quick look around—once he lit that fuse line, Fargo intended to throw caution to the wind and run like hell.

He fished a lucifer from the doeskin possibles bag on his belt and struck it to life on the side of the shack.

"Stand by for a blast—I hope," he muttered aloud as he dropped the burning match onto the line of powder.

Sparks snapped and leapt. Fargo spun on his heel and raced toward the wooded ridge and his Ovaro. A sentry spotted him and shouted: "Halt, whoever the hell you are, or you're buzzard bait!"

In another few seconds, if that powder was good, the sentries would indeed have a far greater distraction on their minds than one running man.

But if that can's a dud, Fargo told himself, then *I'll* be the only show in town.

"Maybe Hollis is right about this stranger," Cas Merrill remarked, peering down into the pitfall trap. "Lookit there! Somehow he missed them stakes. And you can see where he dug holes to climb out."

Boyd Lofley stood beside him, holding a burning pine bough for light. "Yeah. And look what he done to that snake you tossed in for insurance. This jasper ain't no dough belly from the city, uh?"

"That's for *damn* sure." Cas glanced around them, his blunt face suspicious. "But the thing is, where the hell is he? He can't be far away—that snake blood ain't even started to crust up yet. But if he'd've stayed on the trail, we woulda run into him."

Boyd tossed the burning bough into the pit. "That rings right. I say he got hurt in the fall and crawled off nearby. Or maybe he's just trying to fox us by hiding."

Cas nodded, drawing his eight-shot Smith & Wesson to check the loads. "Why'n't we beat the bushes a little? You know that stranger wouldn't point his bridle in this direction 'less he was going after help. Hollis will piss blood if he hears about this."

Boyd, fancy silver spurs chinging, returned to his horse for his percussion-action Sharps.

"I'll search this side of the trail," he called back. "You check the creek side."

Cas headed off into the thick pines. He walked stiff-legged from the time he caught his spur in a cinch and his horse went over on his left leg, crushing it.

For nearly an hour both men searched thoroughly, calling out to each other from time to time. Cas's furrowed scar was ugly in the revealing flashes of lightning that had begun to illuminate the canyon.

"Let's whack the cork for now!" he finally called over to Boyd. "We best go tell Mitt the bad news. He's gonna ream us a new one."

Both men had just swung into the saddle when a cracking, ground-shuddering explosion rent the silence of the night and spooked their mounts. Ahead of them, from the exact direction of the Alliance Mine, a yellow-orange geyser of flame erupted straight up into the sky like the fiery belch of an angry volcano.

"Bleedin' Holy Ghost!" Cas exclaimed. "There goes the mine! C'mon!"

He got his piebald settled down and sank steel into its shoulders, the gelding leaping forward. Behind him, Boyd Lofley gouged his dun with those four-inch rowels. The fiery geyser soon settled somewhat, but the cracking boom of the explosion was still echoing through the Black Hills like a long, ominous rumble of thunder.

By the time the sun broke over the eastern flats, Fargo was well clear of the Alliance claim without incident. Maybe that explosion, he decided, had accomplished his goal of drawing off the hired killers. But it was daylight now, and he had to keep riding, fully exposed, if there was to be any chance of saving those sick prospectors and their families. By Fargo's reckoning, he had already used up about eighteen hours worth of his three-day deadline.

Daybreak found him bearing southeast along Spearfish Creek. The vast Limestone Plateau lay to his right, forcing him to pull down his hat against the swirling dust. Folds of forested peaks ascended to his left. Despite his good start, he assumed the Alliance would have outriders posted throughout the entire Black Hills region.

Even amidst so much danger, however, the eerie beauty of the place commanded his attention. He could see early morning fog on the surrounding mountains, a shifting saddle of pure white cotton against those dark slopes. In places, the grass grew so tall it shined his boots when he rode through it. The pleasant, lazy chuckle of the nearby creek and the dusty twang of grasshoppers' wings made him wish he could stop and sleep.

But by midmorning the overcast sky had turned the color of pewter, and the peace and beauty of the day had given way to sweaty toil. Twice, thanks to rockslides, he had been forced to the grueling task of rolling boulders out of the trail. His stallion could have leaped the obstacles, but Fargo didn't like the gamble—if his pinto came up lame, those fever victims didn't stand a snowball's chance.

Otherwise he stopped only to reset his saddle or briefly spell the Ovaro in a lush patch of bunch grass. He even ate in the saddle, a few bites now and then from his meager rations of hardtack and dried fruit.

Anytime he spotted tracks Fargo dismounted and carefully checked the bend of the grass to see how recent they were. Not surprisingly, he found signs of the Sioux everywhere, many of them recent.

He had not actually spotted any braves since liberating his horse from those two glory-seeking youths. But he knew the Sioux were watching him and everything that was going on in their beloved *Paha Sapa*. He also knew that too many whites still refused to believe that wild savages could be canny warriors—a mistake he never made.

As if timed to verify his thinking, a rifle suddenly spoke its piece behind him.

The bullet whined past his left ear, missing by inches, and kicked up a divot of grass out ahead of him.

"Let's get out of the weather, boy!" he shouted to the stallion.

The Ovaro flinched, but quickly recovered and broke into a run. Fargo lowered his profile and slued around in the saddle, searching for a target behind him.

Another shot, another piercing whine so close that it went on ringing in his eardrums. Fargo spotted a brief curl of blue-white muzzle smoke, but not the shooter. Still, he had enough of a bead to perhaps worry the ambusher and throw off his aim. Fargo whipped his Henry out of its boot and worked the lever even as a third shot nicked one of his stirrup flaps.

He swung down and fired from under the Ovaro's neck, snap-shooting, firing for cover, not the kill. He sprayed the wooded patch around that muzzle smoke, cocking and firing the Henry with one arm, clinging to the Ovaro with the other.

His pattern of bullets evidently had some effect, for no more rounds came chasing after him. Good thing, too, because the Ovaro's mane was matted with sweat, causing Fargo to lose his grip.

He led his stallion to the creek and dropped the bridle so he could drink. The Trailsman's slitted gaze scanned the canyon slopes, watching for reflections. He put himself in the shooter's place, trying to pinpoint tempting locations for a dry-gulcher. Whoever had just shot at him, Fargo assumed he was on the Alliance payroll—most Sioux, except for renegades, rarely attacked from ambush and took pride in facing down a foe.

The next hour or so was uneventful, and Fargo made good time by holding the Ovaro between a trot and a lope. The pinto still showed good bottom and held the pace easily. Where Spearfish Creek took a sharp turn to the West, Fargo continued angling southeast, intending to turn due south when he reached the North Fork River.

The moment the Ovaro's ears pricked forward, Fargo reined in to study the slopes.

"Perhaps the man you seek is close enough to kill you, hair face!"

The Ovaro danced, startled by the voice and ready to break. Fargo laid a hand on his neck, calming him.

"Maybe he is, at that," he replied to the hidden brave, whose skill with English was impressive—and curious.

"Yet, still no weapon in your hand? You, the great hair-face whose deeds even red men sing of?"

"Don't see the need, at the moment," Fargo said. "You're a Lakota and likely you respect the rules of this place. If you decide to *try* killing me, you'll face me first."

He was careful to avoid the word Sioux, "snake in the grass," a name given to the Lakota people by their enemies. The unseen brave laughed—another curious fact, in Fargo's experience. With each other, yes, often, but not in front of enemies such as white men.

"You are confident but do not boast," the brave replied. "To a Lakota, such modesty is for young girls! You wear no coup feathers, Trailsman, yet your war bonnet would trail on the ground. If I do decide to kill you, I will do you the honor of singing my own death song first as a precaution. You would not be an easy kill."

A hawk-nosed brave astride a handsome little strawberry roan emerged from the pines just ahead, turning his pony so he faced Fargo on the narrow trail.

"I am called Kills in Water. I live with a band under the leader Spotted Tail. You can see that I have no weapon but my knife. The coward who shot at you is a disgraced renegade, hired by *your* own whiteskin tribe."

"By Hollis Blackburn, you mean."

The brave nodded. "Some of my people call him the man from the land of the grandmother queen."

"That ain't my tribe. That's England. They were sent packing once, but some have come back to torment us."

Kills in Water shrugged. "You are all *wasichu* to us, whiteskins. Men like him are loyal to no tribe. I call him the Vulture God because wherever he goes, the carrion birds follow. Even worse, he is *witko*, crazy. He kills with no respect for the importance of dying."

"Yeah, I've noticed that," Fargo agreed wryly. "Just like

I've noticed you speak my tongue pretty good, though you seem a mite rusty."

Kills in Water ignored that. "It was the white man's pox," he said, "that wiped out the Rees and the Blackfeet. Now you whites are even killing your own with pox. That is why we Lakota are holding back from attacking all the gold seekers in Spearfish Canyon—we will let the whiteskins kill each other off first. *Then* we will strike."

"The red men have plenty of cold-blooded killers, too," Fargo replied. "And when you ain't making war on whites, you attack other red men. Those you don't kill you turn into slaves. There's good men and bad men, period. Skin color ain't nothing to the matter."

In fact, Fargo wondered, what was the point of this brave's having stopped him? Surely not to discuss the various causes of the wind. His eyes narrowed slightly in speculation as he studied the warrior.

"Seems I recall something I once heard," he remarked, "about a Lakota child who was rescued by white missionaries after bluecoat pony soldiers wiped out his village. He lived with them five years or so. Learned the white man's tongue and their customs. Then he was stolen back by his own people. I don't recall his name, but I hear he's become a fearsome warrior. Greatly respected by the cavalry."

At mention of the cavalry, Kills in Water spat with contempt. "The yellow legs are not warriors, but butchers. As for this Lakota you say lived with whiteskins: Do you see how he would be tainted when his people took him back?"

Fargo nodded, beginning to understand. "He would carry the white man's stink that scares away the buffalo. He would have to become bolder, stronger, more reckless in battle than other braves, all to prove his loyalty and worth."

Kills in Water nodded. "As you say. And perhaps this brave, because he once lived with good whiteskins, would feel some secret pity in his heart for those whites the Vulture God is now trying to kill—especially the children. But do you see? He would be a traitor to his own people, if he tried to help them. Yet, when he sees someone like you helping them, perhaps this brave might decide to at least warn you. A massive attack is coming very soon now, and *all* the gold seekers will be massacred. Unless they leave the *Paha Sapa* soon. Only the All Maker could stop it now."

"How soon?"

Kills in Water only shook his head. "I *would* be a traitor to say more. I look forward to killing the Vulture God and his lick-spittles, but not the others. However, once the war cry sounds, the bloodletting will begin. Seven separate bands of Lakota, including mine, will strike. And once they do, may your God have mercy on any *wasichu* still left in the *Paha Sapa*."

A moment later Kills in Water was gone, swallowed up again by the trees. His warning only confirmed what Fargo had tried to impress upon Elijah and Pow: the urgent need to get out of these disputed mountains as soon as possible.

However, at the moment that need was superseded by another: helping the fever victims before it was too late. And despite the challenge of reaching Shoshone Falls alive, an even harder task lay ahead for Fargo: getting a doctor and supplies *back* to Busted Hump through a deadly gauntlet of hired killers and angry Sioux.

"Pile on the agony," he muttered as he kneed the Ovaro forward toward Thunderhead Mountain.

6

Shoshone Falls had begun in the early 1850s as a Black Hills relay station on the Fort Pierre to Fort Laramie stage route. By now, much to the chagrin of the Sioux Nation, it was on the verge of becoming a permanent settlement.

The reason could be summed up in one little four-letter word: gold. And with the arrival of miners and prospectors came the whores and stores, the gamblers and saloons and grifters. Prices were soon drastically inflated: fifty cents for an egg, three dollars for a pound of butter. Folks there had money to burn, and drunk prospectors often paid for their beer in pinches of gold dust worth hundreds.

Despite its dangerous location, the profit potential of Shoshone Falls eventually even lured a physician, Doctor Joshua Boone, a former U.S. Army contract surgeon who had been summarily dismissed for "inveterate drunkenness."

Boone had a younger sister in Missouri who had died of childbed fever after giving birth to her only child, Colleen. When Colleen's father was killed in a steamboat explosion on the Mississippi twelve years later, the orphaned girl was sent out West to live with her Uncle Josh. She had become a godsend to her uncle because, besides shaping up into a beautiful young woman, she was bright and a fast learner. In the nine years Colleen had lived with him she had become Boone's capable nurse. This allowed him even more luxury to tipple.

Despite his cantankerous personality, Doc Boone loved his niece and treated her well. Except for the frustrating fact, Colleen lamented as she escorted a patient into the side parlor and examination room, that Uncle Josh would tolerate no tomfoolery where men were concerned. He was obsessed with keeping "your virtue *and* your hymen intact, young woman." God help me, she often reminded herself, if he ever finds out it's too late to save my virginity.

"Dang, you look pretty as four aces, Miss Colleen," a young messenger rider named Lincoln West assured her. His hungry eyes feasted on the nubile nurse.

She wore a pinch-waisted blue dress with a lace flounce, her shiny hair in two thick plaits the color of rich cinnamon. Colleen had a pretty, oval face and was built so fetchingly that people assumed she was laced tightly into a corset. But she didn't even own one.

"You'd be wise to lower your voice, Link," she advised her patient. "Uncle Josh's room is close, and he's a light sleeper when men are around me. You'd also be wise to quit brawling in saloons."

She treated the cuts and bruises on his chest and arms with powdered alum. He's a little scrawny, she told herself, but nice dimples. And at least he smells better than most of the men in this frontier money mill. . . .

"What's that old coot's gripe, anyhow?" West groused. "He got a burr under his blanket? Last time I even smiled at you, he dang near aired me out. Heck, you ain't no baby in three-cornered britches. You're a full-growed woman. And brother, *what* a woman!"

"I'd hush that talk, Link," she warned again, although she flushed a little at the welcome compliment. Colleen liked it when men looked at her with desire—the right men, anyhow.

"I *won't* hush," he said in a sudden welter of passion as he reached out to draw her close. "I got a powerful hunger, Colleen."

Both Colleen and West flinched violently at the sound of a gravel-pan voice in the doorway behind them.

"Good, Link, 'cause I'm about to fill your belly for you, you conniving little stag in rut!"

Joshua Boone, wearing nothing but sagging long-handles, stood scowling in the doorway, a scattergun propped in the crook of his left arm. Doc Boone was a short, portly, bald-headed man with scruffy chin whiskers the color of granite. He was surly all the time, but especially when he was hung-over (which he usually was) and his bunions were giving him hell (which they usually were).

But it was his shotgun that Lincoln West noticed most. Everybody knew that Doc kept his scattergun loaded with 20-gauge bird shot—not usually fatal, for men. But it had been known to scare off a few bullyboys, and especially, bedroom bird dogs after his niece.

"Doc, come down off your hind legs," West stammered out. "I was just talking about *food* hunger, is all. You know? Long time since my last meal?"

"Sure, I know—I saw how you just now grabbed for a couple ripe melons, you're so starved."

"Uncle Josh!" Colleen protested. "No need to be coarse."

"Now look-a-here, Doc," West protested, fingers fumbling as he buttoned his shirt back on, "you hadn't oughta wave that artillery piece around like that. If it goes off in here, your niece could get hurt."

"You're right, son." Doc Boone limped across the clean jute rug and opened an equipment cabinet behind the Franklin stove. When he turned around, he brandished the lancet he used to bleed patients.

"One good swipe with this will turn a rooster into a capon!"

"Thanks a bunch, Miss Colleen," West blurted out, shoving a gold piece into her hand. "You're a real fine nurse. Doc, you take care, hear?"

He had change coming but didn't wait around to collect it. After he hurried out, Colleen scowled at her uncle.

"My stars, Uncle Josh! That vulgar mouth of yours! Weren't you ever baptized?"

"I believe so. But the water must not've been hot enough because it didn't take."

"Now it's blasphemy, too! Well, you've got practically every man in this area afraid to even *look* at me."

He nodded, satisfied with that. "Good. Looking leads to touching. And touching leads to a swollen belly. Your mother wasn't an old reprobate like me, Colleen. She was a fine Christian woman who would have raised you proper and decent had she lived. Any man who wants to enjoy *your* favors, missy, will ask for your hand in marriage first."

"Several have," she reminded him, "and you ran them off, too."

"Damn right! I won't have my niece taking up with common riffraff, that's why. Drifters, prospectors, express guards, gamblers—they got one thing on their minds when they look at you. Once they've enjoyed it a few weeks, they'll fade into the sun. No! You'll marry a solid, respectable man of property. A man with deep roots someplace. And I intend to make sure he discovers no nasty surprises on his wedding night."

Doc Boone wagged his scattergun. "I owe it to the memory of your mother, may she rest in peace. You mark my words, girl: God help *any* man I catch trying to compromise your virtue!"

It was early evening when Skye Fargo finally circled the base of Thunderhead Mountain and caught his first view of Shoshone Falls. Dust hazed the little teacup-shaped hollow it sat in.

He had encountered no further trouble since the ambush attempt earlier today. But he was not ruling out the possibility that Hollis Blackburn had mirror-relay stations in place. Which meant he'd likely have a man or two waiting in town for the Trailsman. Fargo figured he was down to about forty hours now on his deadline. Any major delays, from here on out, could spell certain death for many fever victims up north in Busted Hump. Including Elijah and Dotty Stone's little boy, Jimmy.

Although it wasn't even dark yet, Shoshone Falls was already bustling as only a boomtown could. The tinkling notes of a player piano reached Fargo on the wind, along with the sound of raucous shouts, seductive feminine laughter, even a gunshot now and then.

The street was thick with activity when he rode in along the settlement's only road, which was still muddy from a recent rain shower. Few people even bothered to glance at the buckskin-clad rider on the handsome pinto stallion.

The town hadn't progressed to boardwalks yet, only rammed-dirt sidewalks. But there were a few new redbrick buildings with iron shutters painted black. Fargo noted a harness shop, a fairly big mercantile, a smithy, an assay office. He also spotted a freight office with mail sacks stacked on the loading dock. The Overland Mail had been established by Butterfield in 1858, but mail tended to pile up, waiting on good weather or available drivers.

A hell-and-damnation preacher raved in the street, no one paying any attention to him. Not surprisingly, there were several thirst parlors in town. Fargo picked the one with the most horses hitched to the tie rail out front—the Hog's Breath saloon. Weary and tailsore from pounding a saddle since yesterday, he reined in and hitched the Ovaro. Fargo needed a quick jolt of whiskey and a little information. He was also curious to see if any interesting characters might mosey into the saloon behind him.

Noise and oily yellow light spilled past the slatted batwings. Fargo slapped them open and stepped into a smoke-filled bedlam. A faro dealer sat in a half circle of bettors. The case tender called out each card like a circus barker. The only females in this tobacco-reeking place were a few soiled doves who looked like they'd been rode hard and put away wet.

Brass cuspidors were placed all around, but the condition of the sawdust-sprinkled floor proved few ever hit them. Along a side wall, a few battered billiard tables sported bullet holes and patched felts.

As he bellied up to the bar, Fargo's eyes shifted to the greasy back-bar mirror. The next person to enter, after him, was a half-breed wearing dirty sailcloth trousers and a beaded shirt, his dark hair cut raggedly short. He headed toward the opposite end of the bar.

"Whiskey," Fargo told the bar dog. "And can you tell me where to find the doctor?"

" 'Bout this time of day," the man replied, "you'll find him on his face dead drunk."

"Quite the drinking man, is he?"

"Mister, Doc Boone don't just *drink*. It's like his legs are pipes through the floor. He ain't a half-bad pill roller if you can catch him sober. Good thing his niece is also his nurse—she usually does most of the doctorin'. Once you've seen her, mister, you'll look for ways to get sick."

"Where's the office?"

"You can't miss it. Head west out of town, it's just past the feed stable. A solid wooden house with fancy gingerbread work under the eaves."

Fargo nodded, still watching that half-breed. He seemed to be looking everywhere but in this direction.

Fargo tossed back his drink. It was cheap panther piss that started burning the second it hit his belly. But he wanted to keep the bartender around, so he nodded for a refill.

"Who's the 'breed being served at the other end of the bar?" he inquired.

"Calls himself Coyote, and he's a good man to let alone. Cold-blooded killer. Dame Rumor has it he's planted over a dozen men just in the Dakota Territory—none of 'em self-defense, if you catch my drift?"

"You got law here?"

The bar dog snorted. "Vigilante bunch who call themselves Regulators. Mostly they just roll drunks and collect 'fines.' Ain't a one of 'em with the oysters to brace Coyote. You just try looking into his eyes—dead as stones. That bastard ain't even got a soul."

"Souls ain't my line," Fargo pointed out. "But he looks like a hard twist, all right."

Despite the time pressure, Fargo knew both he and the Ovaro eventually had to rest up for a few hours. Neither man nor beast had slept for nearly two days now—two very grueling days. And no doubt the return trip would prove far more harrowing, especially after that spectacular explosion last night. Nor could he forget Kills in Water's ominous warning. This was no time to fall asleep in the saddle.

"One more question, bottles, then I'll sew my lips shut. Got a flophouse around here? I just need a little shut-eye before I move on."

"We got what you might call a hotel. But my brother owns it, so I happen to know it's plumb full up. But you can still buy a hot bath there. And for sleep, you can rent a hay stall at the feed stable. Three hours for three dollars."

Fargo whistled. "Three dollars for a stable nap! Hell, I can get a hotel room for all night, anywhere in the West, for two bucks."

"Not here, chum. Hotel room is six bucks a night. Just like them two shots just cost you six bits apiece. Any complaints, go talk to the Swede."

He rolled his head toward a huge man mountain who was seated on a raised platform at the back of the barroom. A sawed-off cue stick dangled from his wrist on a leather thong.

Fargo grinned. "A buck-and-a-half sounds more than fair to me. Keep the change."

He left the pouch of gold Elijah had given him alone, flipping two silver dollars onto the plank bar. The half-breed continued to studiously ignore him as Fargo strolled outside into the gathering darkness.

He rode the tired and hungry Ovaro through town to the feed stable at the outskirts. The hostler had left a note saying he was at supper. So for now Fargo unsaddled his horse and turned him into the corral. Then he tossed a pitchfork load of hay over the fence.

He went inside and tossed his saddle on a rack in the tack room. He also left money and a note instructing that the Ovaro be curried, rubbed down, and given a good feed of oats and crushed barley.

Before he walked next door to the doctor's house, Fargo took time to return to the corral for a quick inspection of the Ovaro's hoofs, feet, and fetlocks. At one point he glanced toward the apron of shadow across the street and thought he glimpsed those familiar sailcloth trousers.

"Looks like the man with no soul has taken an interest in us, boy," he remarked quietly to his horse. "I predict things will get mighty lively around here in a hurry."

"Dag'gum, Fargo!" exclaimed Joshua Boone when his visitor had explained the emergency. "Is your wick flickering, son? I'm too damn old to go gallavantin' off through the heart of the Black Hills. The Sioux are packed in there tighter than maggots in moldy meat. I'm sorry about the plight of those prospectors. I truly am. But they brought it on themselves."

"That's just it," Fargo gainsaid. "They *didn't* bring it on themselves. Sure, they're stupid for being there in the first place. But they were deliberately infected with mountain fever. And the culprits are not the Sioux."

"You can prove all this?"

Fargo shook his head. "Not so's it would convince the law—not yet, anyhow. Assuming there was any law up there. But I'll get that proof."

Doc Boone's only response to this was a long, agonized groan. He was leaning over the Franklin stove to inhale herbal steam from a vaporizer.

"He's curing a . . . headache," Colleen whispered to their handsome visitor.

"Actually the word is hangover," Doc Boone corrected his niece in a voice like a deathbed croak. "I ain't ashamed I'm a drunk, this ain't Boston. And *please* don't shout like that, Colleen. My head is throbbing like a war drum."

"You've got the right medicine to cure mountain fever, haven't you?" Fargo pressed.

"That ain't the problem. They'll need diluted carbolic to treat the disease, and laudanum so they can sleep after the treatment. I've got plenty of both. But we'll never get it to them in time."

"I'll get you there," Fargo said confidently.

"What, clear up to Ragged Top Mountain? Why, that's all the way to the other end of the Black Hills. A man might's well enter the first circle of hell!"

"I'll get you there," Fargo repeated.

"In a pig's eye you will! And even if you did, who knows how many more will be sick by the time we get there? I couldn't treat them all without help, which would mean taking Colleen into the heart of the Sioux stronghold. I'm dead set against it. You got any notion what them red devils would do to a female captive as pretty as my niece?"

Doc Boone paused to send a suspicious glance at Fargo. Ever since the bearded stranger had arrived, he and Colleen had been trading "smoldering glances."

"Not to mention," Boone added, "what *you* obviously hope to do to her."

"I'd rather leave her. But if she has to go, I promise to protect both of you. And you'd be well paid for your trouble, Doc."

"Huh! Fellow, it would cost you dear to lure me into the northern Black Hills. You ain't got that kind of money."

Doc Boone's eyes narrowed in suspicion. "Besides, you look like a debt skipper, to me. Or an army deserter—we get plenty of them around here. I won't accept any more of that damn U.S. script, if that's what you got. That's for soldiers. I want money that spends."

"You mean, money like this?"

Fargo took out the bulging pouch of gold and shook several large nuggets out into his hand.

Doc Boone's red-streaked eyes bulged at the sight. He scratched at his scruffy chin whiskers, eyeing the color in Fargo's callused palm. Finally, he removed a thin silver flask from his coat pocket.

"Uncle Josh," Colleen protested, "you're still recovering from last night, you—"

"Just a nip to wash my teeth," he assured her, still staring covetously at that gold. He tossed back a swallow and added, "Of course, I *did* take an oath, didn't I? Help my fellow man, all that."

"*That's* the spirit," Fargo said, thumping him on the back and then catching him quickly before he fell. "But you two would have to be ready to hit the trail soon—in a few hours, at most. I need to see about buying supplies and a wagon and team to haul them. Then I have to catch forty winks. I'll stop by for you when I'm ready.

"But, Mr. Fargo," Colleen protested, watching him from eyes the color of sunlit honey. "Tomorrow is Sunday. Don't you keep the Sabbath?"

"I don't generally know what day of the week it is," he

admitted. "And sometimes I even have to guess the month. But does keeping the Sabbath include allowing fellow Christians to die?"

"No, of course not. But . . . well, what about accommodations?"

"Accommodations?" Fargo repeated as if it were a foreign word.

"Well, yes. For one thing, where will we sleep?"

"Likely we won't," Fargo admitted. "If we have to, it'll be in a Tucson bed."

Her pretty face scrunched up in puzzlement. "What in the world is a Tucson bed?"

Fargo grinned. She was an easy mark. "You lie on your stomach and cover that with your back."

"H'ar now!" Doc Boone cut in. "You'll launder your speech around my niece, Fargo. No more talk of beds and stomachs and lying down, hear me? I swear on her mother's memory, you lay one horny hand on Colleen, and I'll send you across the Great Divide!"

Fargo's first stop, after leaving Doc Boone's place, was the mercantile store. He waited impatiently while a slow-moving clerk in sleeve garters cut a dollar's worth off a coil of strong rope for another customer.

"Sorry, mister," the clerk informed him when Fargo stepped up to the counter. "It's already past closing time."

But once Fargo flashed his gold, explaining he needed a large order, the clerk gladly agreed to put together a special order of supplies.

Fargo ordered flour, bacon, sugar, beans, salt, corn meal, coffee, and jerked beef. The items included sassafras candy for the kids and peaches and tomatoes packed in the new tin airtights.

Keeping his eyes peeled for the half-breed named Coyote, Fargo next returned to the feed stable. His Ovaro had been well tended to by a cheerful, nearly toothless old hostler wearing a beaver hat.

"I need a team and a conveyance, old timer, right away. I've got supplies to haul. Got anything to sell me?"

The old codger dug at his armpit, thinking. "I got me an old supply wagon around back, needs a little axle grease, is all. We can dicker on that. But a team, that's a real poser. Good horseflesh comes scarce in these parts—hell, I could sell that fine pinto of yours right now for five hunnert, cash on the barrelhead."

"I'm buying, not selling."

"Uh huh. Well, 'bout all I got is them two blood bays in the last stall. I won't try to hornswaggle you, young feller. Now, I ain't saying they're buckets of glue. But they've seen hard use, and neither animal is a spring chicken anymore. And they've been stall-fed so long, they've got lazy."

Fargo walked down to examine the horses. Both geldings had deep girth galls and gaping saddle sores. He felt a moment's anger when he saw the scars on both animals's shoulders. He could not tolerate a man spurring a horse in the shoulders.

"These are riding horses," he pointed out. "I need a team to pull a load."

"Them's combination horses, broke to both saddle and traces."

A quick glance at a horse's teeth would tell its age. Fargo checked both animals and decided they wouldn't drop dead.

"These'll have to do," he said.

They quickly settled on a price.

"You get 'em hitched to that wagon," Fargo said. "Then grease that axle and take the rig over to the mercantile. Tell the clerk to load up the supplies I ordered. I'm going to grab a hot bath and a meal. All right if I come back here and sack out in a stall for an hour or so?"

The old codger chuckled as he patted the pocketful of gold nuggets Fargo had just paid out. "Stranger, considerin' the money you just spent? Hell, come back   d burn the place down, for aught I care."

Fargo headed on foot toward the three-story Crystal Palace, the hotel the bartender had mentioned. He remained vigilant, but hadn't spotted the 'breed since his first trip to the feed stable before full dark set in. That bothered him. It reminded him of a saying about the Apaches down in the Southwest: *Be careful when you see them. Be even more careful when you don't.*

He went around back to the hotel bath house and paid an exorbitant seventy-five cents for a ragged scrap of towel and a chunk of lye soap. A Chinese worker wearing a pig-tail and a floppy blue blouse filled up a wooden tub with steaming-hot water. Fargo had the room to himself, so he was careful to pick a tub with a clear view of the door.

He stripped naked and slid his Colt from its holster, leaving it within handy reach beside the tub. Then he eased into the hot water.

Only now, as the swirling heat relaxed his aching muscles, did Fargo fully realize how tired and sleepy he was. Several times, as he soaked, his eyelids got heavy and he almost nodded off.

Too late, he realized the deadly mistake he'd made.

He felt a sudden, chilly breeze on his back and shoulders—as if, he told himself, someone behind him had just opened a window.

A window . . . only now did he recall he hadn't checked behind the little square of monk's cloth curtain on the back wall.

"Fargo, you damn fool," he chastised himself even as he suddenly dove deep, swallowing a mouthful of soapy water.

The hammering racket of sudden gunfire seemed obscenely loud in the empty room. But the underwater *thuck-foosh* sound of slugs ripping into the full tub was even more magnified, threatening to burst his eardrums.

The first two shots missed him by mere inches, and Fargo knew damn well he'd end up looking like a sieve if he just laid there playing fish in the barrel. Figuring any action was better than none, he gathered his strength and rolled hard to the right, flipping the tub over and washing out onto the floor in a huge splash of sudsy water.

He made a desperate grab for his Colt, got hold of it, and continued rolling fast as bullets stitched holes in the wooden floor just behind him, chasing him toward the wall. Fargo, dripping wet and unable to see clearly with lye soap burning his eyes, came up on his heels fanning the hammer.

The curtain danced and flapped as he blew the window out. He hurried to the shattered opening and peered cautiously out. But if he had hit the shooter, it couldn't be too serious—there was no one in sight, just an empty lot of ankle-high weeds.

Fargo's heart-hammering fear response turned into a slow boil of anger.

"You should have finished the job just now, Coyote," he murmured as he began quickly toweling down. "Because now it's my turn."

7

Hollis Blackburn paced nervously in his den, so upset the face behind his waxed and twirled mustache was tinged pink with angry blood.

"You incompetent chawbacons!" he fumed. "Last night Skye Fargo came within an ace of blowing this entire mining operation to rubble! Good thing we have another cache of powder charges or production would have been disrupted for weeks. And now not *one* of you blockheads can tell me where Fargo is?"

The four blockheads in question were scattered around the den, looking embarrassed, uncomfortable, and surly: Mitt Brennan, Cas Merrill, Orrin Jones, and Boyd Lofley.

"Fargo is raising a fair amount of hell," Mitt conceded.

"*That's* all you can say, Mitt?" Hollis raged on, turning to glare at his mine captain. He mocked Brennan with his own words from yesterday: " 'We'll get the net around that son of a bitch.' You fools couldn't locate your own asses in a hall of mirrors!"

Hollis was so agitated he wasn't even bothering with his usual pretense of giving "indirect orders" and speaking in veiled references.

"By now," he added, "he may well have made it to Shoshone Falls and a doctor. I have faith in Coyote's . . . talents. But Fargo is obviously a match for any mother's son. We can't assume he won't make it back. And I'm warning all of you now. We may *all* end up kicking at air if any of those prospectors make it out of the Black Hills to tell their story. Since we can't mend it, we'll have to *end* it."

Hollis paused in the embrasure of a big bay window, gazing down on the moonlit mining operation. He removed the silver snuffbox tucked into his sleeve and wedged a pinch of snuff behind his upper lip.

"More smokestacks and businessmen," he muttered as if the rest of the men weren't there. "That's what the American West needs—not these strutting peacock crusaders like Fargo."

Cas Merrill stroked the knife scar on his right cheek. "Ah, you're building a pimple into a peak, Mr. Blackburn. Don't you fret none about Fargo. If he slips past Coyote, we'll give 'm what-for. By the bye—is that little Frenchie gal of yours to home? I dearly love to hear your . . . night woman play the pie-ano. Must be sweet, huh, gettin' it reg-'lar from a nice little piece like her?"

Hollis spun around to stare at his hireling. "Why would you care? Suzette wouldn't let you in the same room with her. She told me you remind her of pig tripes. As for giving Fargo 'what-for'—he's already eluded a mountain top you sent crushing down on him. Somehow he fell into your no-doubt ingenious pitfall and missed the poisoned stakes. An attempt earlier today to ambush him south of here failed. Now it's up to Coyote to kill him. If—*damn* it, Boyd, I asked you to stop that bloody racket!"

Boyd Lofley, as usual, was snapping the wheel of one of his fancy silver spurs with a finger. "Sorry," he muttered. "Nervous habit."

"If Fargo gets back in time with a doctor," Hollis resumed, "we'll never run those shit-heel prospectors out in time. We've got to mine that rich vein they're sitting on and get out of here quick—all reports from our paid renegades indicate the Sioux are organizing a massive force. They intend to purge the Black Hills of all intruders."

Hollis paused to give his next words more weight.

"I'm attempting to placate some of the war chiefs with a load of trade goods, just gain some time to blast out that vein. So it's imperative that we stop Fargo from bringing help. Fever will kill most of those prospectors starting in just a few days. The rest will then be easy to wipe out with a strong strike force. The whole thing can be blamed on the Sioux."

"Wipe out?" Orrin Jones echoed. "What, even the kids?"

Hollis shrugged. "Nits make lice. But the key, again, is stopping Fargo. Mitt?"

"Yo!"

"I want you to start picking men for the strike force. Try to get war veterans and good marksmen. As for our bearded Robin Hood and the question of who kills him . . ."

Hollis removed a small key from his fob pocket and crossed to a cherrywood cabinet beside Orrin Jones's chair. He unlocked it and removed a bulging leather pouch.

"We'll turn that decision over to Judge Moneybags."

Hollis untied the pouch and spilled its contents onto the top of the cabinet. Some of the glittering gold coins bounced off the table and onto the rug.

"Gold double eagles, gentlemen. None of this sloppy guess-work with dust or nuggets. A two-thousand dollar bonus for the man who untethers Skye Fargo from his soul."

All four men stared at the gold. Unlike Hollis they were not the kind with big-scale ambitions. That gold meant a high old time for months: drinking, whoring, and gambling, the luxury of hotel sheets and weekly barbering and restaurant meals and two-bit cigars.

"There's only two ways he can get to Busted Hump in time," Mitt Brennan remarked as he stood up and hitched his gun belt. "The high-country trail or the canyon route. We got 'em both covered. But the high country is rougher, slower going. And he'll have a townie doc with him. He'll likely take the canyon route. He slipped out of our hands once, Mr. Blackburn, but he won't do it again."

Cas Merrill's eyes hadn't left those shiny double eagles since Blackburn spilled them out.

"Matter fact," he said to Hollis, "I mean to make you a trade, boss: them yaller boys there for Skye Fargo's head in a burlap sack."

Fargo quickly checked out the supplies and verified that everything he ordered had been loaded. Then he thumped the wagon gate up and drove the locking pin home.

He tossed his tack into the back of the supply wagon and tied the Ovaro to the tailgate. He made it a loose knot so the Ovaro could pull free in a scrape. While he worked he kept his gaze shifting to all sides. Coyote had failed once, but a killer like that didn't scare off easy. A paid killer had to finish the job or he'd never sleep nights.

As to sleep—Fargo ended up with less than an hour of it, waking up sluggish but quickly shaking out the kinks. At least, he told himself as he climbed up onto the board seat of the wagon, the moon was still in full quarter and a million stars blazed in the sky. If they had to travel after dark, it was a good night for it.

He flipped the reins and the reluctant bays lumbered forward toward Doc Boone's house.

He found the doctor and his niece ready and waiting in a buggy with its top up against the dust.

Fargo touched his hat to Colleen. She had changed into a dark broadcloth skirt and a crisp white shirtwaist. Her bonnet was freshly starched and blocked.

"You almost look too pretty for a rough trip like this," he greeted her.

She sent him a sly, slanted glance. "You wish I was uglier, Mr. Fargo?"

"*Both* of you," Doc Boone exploded, "can just nip this shameless flirting in the bud right now. I'll have my eye on the two of you."

"Well at least," Fargo said, "I see you've left that scattergun of yours to home."

"That's right. It's good for home defense, but inconvenient in this small buggy. On the road, I take my traveling gal, Miss Pepper."

Boone whipped out an old six-shot pepperbox pistol manufactured by Benjamin and Boston Darling. Fargo's eyes widened at the sight of six loaded barrels staring at him.

"*Ho*-ly Hannah!" he exclaimed. "Don't be pointing that old crowd-killer at me! You can't trust that thing, Doc—a weapon that old is bound to have a worn sear. A worn sear makes any gun hair-trigger. And with that pepperbox, you fire one barrel, and all six are likely to go off."

" 'At's right," Boone said. "Makes it easier to hit what you're aiming at. I double hog-tie *dare* you to try bird-dogging my niece—you *will* spring some leaks."

"Don't presume on your gray hairs, old roadster. You've made your point. But don't be aiming a weapon at a man 'less you intend to fire it. It's a quick way to get yourself killed. Let's raise dust."

"One second," the doctor called out just as Fargo started to flick the reins. "I forgot something."

The buggy tilted hard to one side as the portly medico climbed out and hurried up to the house. He stopped once to shout back, "I meant what I said, Fargo! Keep them grabby hands to yourself—an *old* man can pull a trigger, too!"

"Does he just hate me," Fargo asked Colleen, "or does he always watch you like Midas over his gold?"

"He's even worse," she admitted, "when he can tell I especially like a fella. I ain't one to hide it when I do."

Fargo grinned. "That a compliment?"

She lifted her pert little nose higher into the air, playing the haughty miss. "Mr. Fargo, you are impertinent! I didn't say I meant you, did I?"

"What's it matter *who* you meant? Way things appear to me, your uncle makes sure you never get to be alone with a man."

Her snooty face softened and turned a little sly again. "Men *try* to hem us women, don't they? Don't forget, he drinks too much. Passes out a lot. Once in a while I manage to go out . . . picking flowers with some fella I like."

Fargo could see her uncle returning. Colleen hurried up and added: "Maybe sometime *we* could go picking flowers, Mr. Fargo?"

"I'd admire to, Miss Colleen."

Fargo meant it, too, he wasn't just being gallant. She was a tidy little package: pretty, well-built, of age, and eager to play. But he doubted if the opportunity would arise. With Coyote still alive, they faced grave danger behind, and who knew what they might ride into?

"Now I'm ready," Doc Boone said.

He handed his niece two bottles of whiskey.

"That's Tennessee sippin' stock," he told Fargo. "I won't drink Indian-burner like these fools in town."

He grunted as he heaved his bulk back into the buggy. Doc Boone snapped the reins, and the Busted Hump rescue operation was underway.

Especially with a woman going along, Fargo felt it only fair to quickly summarize the dangers before they got too far along on the journey. As soon as they'd cleared town, he pulled alongside them and provided a few more details.

"Whoa!" Doc Boone shouted to his horse, tugging back

on the reins. "Look, Fargo, I knew the Sioux were stirred up. But earlier, you didn't mention any of this about Hollis Blackburn. And *Coyote* is mixed up in it? Why, hell! Is that *all* we got to worry about? Plague, murder, and massacre? I feel blessed!"

"Oh, hush, Uncle Josh, and start driving," Colleen rebuked him gently. "Mr. Fargo will protect us."

"A-huh. He'll gladly throw his body over yours—and mine to the wolves."

But Doc Boone clucked to his horse and they were off again. Fargo pulled on ahead.

"A man like that," Boone remarked to his niece, "is a tomcat on the prowl. You watch him."

"I don't imagine he needs to prowl too far," she replied demurely. "He's too handsome."

"Hunh! Sounds like you're the one I best watch close. You act like a woman with an itch only one man can scratch."

"I asked you to watch that barracks-room talk!"

"Sorry," he mumbled.

But Colleen wasn't really offended because it was true. She smiled in the moonlight. "Just have another drink, Uncle Josh. It'll calm you down."

Fargo bore northwest, keeping Medicine and Copper peaks as his compass points with the Polestar halfway between them. The forested slopes were too dark to show at night, but both peaks carved perfect silhouettes where they blocked out the stars.

He had considered taking the high-country route. Defense would be easier on high ground. But with two conveyances on that narrow trail, rockslides could force them to time-consuming backtracking. So it would have to be the same canyon route he followed on his way south to Shoshone Falls.

Fargo hadn't gotten enough sleep to completely trust his senses. Not with nerveless killing machines like Coyote lurking out there in the darkness. So he employed a trick he'd learned from an old army scout—he removed a plug of tobacco he kept in his saddlebag just for this purpose.

He gnawed off a corner and got it juicing good. Then he smeared some of the juice inside each of his eyelids—just enough harmless but annoying sting to keep him wide awake for hours.

The night was warm but gusty. Wind pressed the grass flat and howled with a mournful sound like souls in torment. Within a few hours Doc Boone had passed out drunk, and Colleen had taken the reins. Now and then the trail widened out, and she would pull up beside Fargo.

"What are you doing in these parts, Skye?" she asked him at one point.

"Oh, I'm just yondering."

"Drifting, you mean. Is that all you ever do?"

"It keeps me busy," he assured her. "Besides—now and again I *drift* right into gals like you."

"Gals like me?" she said, a teasing lilt to her voice. "And just what kind of gal is that?"

"Well, for one thing . . . I notice you don't wear a corset, Miss Colleen. Or need to. But you seem bright, so maybe you can answer a question I've always wondered about?"

"Which is? . . ."

He glanced over at her, grinning. "Is it true what they say—tight lacings kindle impure desires?"

"Why, Mr. Fargo!"

He could almost see her blushing in the moonlight. But a few moments later she replied, "I really couldn't tell you. But certain *men* surely do."

"That's all I needed to hear. I think me and you need to see about picking some flowers, all right—real soon. You agree?"

"As soon as possible. Even sooner."

All this talk, however, had disturbed Doc Boone. His steady snores ceased. In his drunken stupor, he had returned to his days of extended travel with the army.

"Sergeant, it'd be a good idea to send out flankers!" he called out. "You men in the rear—hold wide intervals around that ambulance!"

"Lord, is he drunk," Colleen said. "Thinks he's a field commander now."

Fargo nodded. "He's got a skinful, all right. Can he doctor like this?"

"No. That's why I had to come along. But he thinks he's in charge, or he's too proud to admit he isn't."

Well behind them now, Thunderhead Mountain was still putting on an impressive lightning show. Fargo took advantage of the frequent flashes to scour the surrounding terrain. His Henry lay balanced across his thighs as he drove the supply wagon.

"You expect trouble?" she asked.

"It does seem to dog me," he admitted.

But they made surprisingly good progress without incident. Now and then Fargo reined in to spell the horses and let them drink. Well after midnight, however, they reached a stretch of water-scarce trail he recalled from his first trip. They wouldn't be picking up Spearfish Creek for several hours yet. The nearest water now was Dearfield Lake, not quite the halfway point in their journey.

Fargo reined in, letting Colleen pull up beside him. Doc Boone was still snoring with a racket like a leaky bellows.

"Last chance to water the horses for a spell," he told her. "There's a little seep spring just to our right, behind that stand of jack pine. That ginger of yours is holding up, and my stallion ain't broke a sweat. But this team I'm driving will need to tank up."

The spring was right where Fargo remembered it. But recent rains had left it muddy at its edges.

"Your buggy's light, just let your horse walk right out and drink," Fargo told his pretty companion, handing her down. "But I'll have to unhitch these nags of mine. That wagon will bog down."

Fargo untied the Ovaro. Then he moved around front and unhooked the tug chains from the singletrees before unbuckling the harnesses.

"Skye?"

Her voice was soft beside him, a little husky with urgency. When Fargo turned to look at Colleen, his pulse suddenly quickened. She had unbuttoned the shirtwaist and pulled it open. Only a thin chemise covered the high swell of her breasts. In that clear moonlight, he saw the dark swellings where her nipples dinted the fabric.

"Touch me!" she begged in an urgent whisper. "I need to feel a man's hands on me."

Fargo liked to oblige the opposite sex when he could. His hands cupped the tight heft of her, feeling her nipples immediately stiffen against his palms.

"Let me see if *you* want me," she whispered, one hand sliding across his chest and stomach, going even lower until she had a grip on the hard, throbbing furrow in his trousers.

"Oh, Skye, I've *got* to feel this inside me! Please? Right now?"

Carried away, she simply leaned back against one corner of the supply wagon and hitched up her dress. "*Do* me, Skye! Do me here and now, I'm on fire for you!"

Fargo would have picked a better place and time. Then again, he reasoned, never let it be said he ever sent a starving woman away hungry.

However, even as he fumbled his buckskin trousers open, Fargo watched the Ovaro's head swing up from the water, ears pricked.

Somewhere out there in the moonlit shadows, a twig snapped.

His Colt leaped into his hand, and Colleen gasped with fright. "Skye! What is it?"

He touched a finger to her lips, silencing her. For a long time he listened. But soon the Ovaro was drinking again, and Fargo heard nothing but the wind gusting.

"No time to play," he decided reluctantly as he leathered his Colt. "Let's make tracks."

By the time dawn streaked the eastern horizon pink, Fargo knew his team was played out. But they had made good progress through the night. Dearfield Lake, the halfway point, was only about three hours ahead. With maybe thirty hours or so remaining on his deadline, he was actually making better time than he'd hoped.

He glanced carefully around in the gathering light of daybreak. They had entered a stretch of scant-grown hills, allowing him to breathe a little easier. Coyote, and whoever else might be trying to kill him, would not be likely to strike here where cover was scarce. Not with prime ambush country just ahead.

He glanced back at the buggy. Doc Boone was still out cold, snoring with a racket fit to scare off the Wendigo. Poor Colleen, who'd been stuck with the driving all night, kept nodding out from exhaustion.

Fargo pulled back on the reins, letting her catch up.

"My horses are done in," he told her. "And so are you. Since we're making good time, and I just spotted water, we'll break here for one hour. I'll stand watch while you grab a nap."

Colleen was too tired to argue. "Where's this water?" she asked. "I need to freshen up."

"Over there," he said, pointing to a muddy pool a few yards off the trail.

"Skye, we can't drink that!" she protested. "Or wash in it, either. Why, it looks like brown gravy."

"We won't have to drink it. I'll show you a trick, greenhorn."

Fargo stopped a few feet back from the edge of the pool. Quickly, he used his hands to scoop out a hole in the soft dirt. The ground-filtered water that soon seeped in to fill the new hole was almost clear. He scooped out another hole nearby.

Colleen drank and quickly washed up while Fargo spread his groundsheet and blanket out for her. Then, while she curled up for some blessed sleep, he took turns unhitching and leading the horses to his new water holes. It grew lighter as he worked, and Fargo never stopped studying the surrounding terrain.

He, too, was exhausted, having slept about one hour in the past three days or so. The Ovaro, least spent of the horses, drank last. Fargo watched the stallion stretch his neck toward the little pool, drinking, the muscles sharply defined in the early light.

"Join me if you want to, Skye," Colleen's sleepy whisper reached him from her grassy spot between the buggy and the wagon.

"If I was ever tempted," Fargo replied, hot images giving him a sudden flush of lustful heat. "But we better not. I'd take my chances if it was just your uncle's pepperbox. Coyote is another story. *He* ain't drunk nor sleeping, I'd wager."

"Oh, all right. But you owe me something . . . sweet," she mumbled even as she nodded out.

Fargo, his rump sore from the hard board seat, settled with his back propped against one of the wagon wheels. He kept his Henry to hand as he willed himself to stay awake. Doc Boone, meantime, snored steadily on, oblivious as a baby.

The sun finally cleared the peaks to the east, and full light had arrived.

"Doc, you old scutter, wake up and wipe the drool off your chin!" Fargo called out as he stood up, brushing sand off his trousers and stretching his back. "Colleen, rise and shine, pretty lady!"

But a quick glance in her direction told Fargo she was already awake—wide awake and so scared her pretty face was pale as new linen. She lay wrapped in his blanket, not moving a muscle.

"What's wrong?" he called over to her.

Her eyes looked big as silver dollars. "Help!" she whispered. "For God's sake, help me! There's a snake curled up against me!"

"Stop talking," Fargo commanded. "It crawled into your blanket to get warm. The vibrations from your voice will wake it up. Don't move! Don't even twitch an eyelid."

Walking lightly on the balls of his feet, Fargo crossed to her and knelt on one knee. He could see the lump where the snake had coiled up on her stomach.

Carefully, he picked up one corner of the blanket and peeked under it. His lips started to tug into a grin at what he saw. Instead, he forced a serious look.

"Easy, girl," he advised her. "Be strong. It's just as I feared—a big old rattlesnake."

Her face drained from pale to chalk white.

"You just lay still and ignore whatever I do," he told her. "This will be a tricky piece of work. I've done it before, but it will require your full cooperation."

Beginning at her right ankle, Fargo poked one hand under the blanket and began sliding the hand up her shapely leg.

He took his time gliding over the supple calf, even more time when he reached her satiny inner thigh. He stroked her slow and soft.

"That's—that's awful nice," she stammered. "But won't it anger the rattler?"

"Shush, girl! I'm puttin' it in a trance."

Higher and higher his hand moved on her inner thigh, stroking, petting in slow circles. Against her will, Colleen had started to squirm her hips a little, unable to contain the tickling pleasure building in her loins.

Fargo inched higher, felt sudden heat and moist, chamois-soft lips that opened for his fingers like petals to sunshine.

Colleen gasped, her eyes glazed with pleasure.

73

"That snake must be close now," he whispered, moving his fingers faster. "You think?"

"Vuh-very close," she managed. "Oh, yes, *close!*"

"Then I guess I better stop."

"Skye Fargo, don't you *dare* stop!"

"But, honey, that rattlesnake—"

"—is in a trance by now! And so am I. *Please*, Skye, keep doing what you were doing?"

Fargo gladly obliged, his busy fingers cosseting her love nest. But the pleasure waves were too much for Colleen. Her whimpers built into a sharp little yipping cry of delight as she climaxed.

"There goes *your* spot in heaven," Fargo teased her.

"It was worth it," she said on a sigh.

But her passionate outcry had finally roused Doc Boone from his slumber. The first thing he saw, as his eyes snapped open, was his niece lying on the ground wrapped in a blanket. And Skye Fargo kneeling beside her, his arm way up inside that blanket!

"Fargo, by eternal thunder, I'll blow you to perdition, you sneaking son of a whore!"

Boone struggled down from the buggy, waving his old pepperbox pistol as he stalked closer, murder in his eyes.

"Simmer down, you old jackass," Fargo snapped. "Your niece has got a snake in her bedroll."

"My sweet aunt! She's got a snake's *hand* in her bedroll. You're molesting my niece while she sleeps!"

"No, Uncle Josh!" Colleen cried out. "There's a rattlesnake coiled on me!"

Boone had reached them now. "Snake, huh? Then how come your face is all flushed and you're breathing like a whore at high tide?"

"She's scared, you drunken old sot," Fargo replied, "because *this* woke her up."

Fargo had known, since that first peek, that it was just a harmless grass snake. But Doc Boone had no time to get a good look at the serpent Fargo suddenly whipped out and flung into Boone's face.

"Great day in the morning!"

Boone staggered sideways, plopped into the mud hole, and accidentally discharged his pepperbox. As Fargo had predicted, all six barrels shot their charges. Instantly, one entire side of the buggy's canvas top was shredded to tatters.

Doc Boone thrashed around in the shallow mud hole like a beached whale, firing off a string of curses that would make a horse blush. Fargo, despite his exhaustion, laughed so hard he had to sink to his knees.

Colleen rose from her bed, pleasure-gazed eyes watching Fargo.

"That was mighty nice," she told him as her uncle sputtered on. "But I hope you don't expect to leave it at that?"

"Not even if it costs me six bullet holes in my sitter, sugar plum," he assured her.

Fargo went over to help fish Doc Boone out of the soup.

"Fargo, you skirt-chasing quiff hound, I'll—"

"Now, Doc," Fargo cut in, his tone brooking no nonsense, "this ain't the time nor the place for such high-handed carrying on. I ain't keen on the idea of thumping an elderly gent. But I will if you keep pushing it. *Don't* be pointing Miss Pepper at me like that."

"Uncle Josh will be fine," Colleen soothed, using an old rag to swipe at the mud coating him. "He's just cranky from the trip. Once he has a bite to—"

"Don't coddle me, Colleen! That man had his hand up your dress, and you let him! He—"

If Doc Boone finished his sentence, Fargo never heard it. Just then a hidden rifle barked, the sound reaching them a split second after the bullet ripped into Fargo's flesh.

8

"If you looked any lower," Powhatan Stone greeted his brother, "you'd be walking on your lower lip."

"If I *felt* any lower," Elijah replied, "I'd blow my own brains out."

It was just daybreak. Pow had come down to check on the pesthouse patients just as Elijah was leaving. The two men stood about thirty feet away from the crude log structure, eyes warily scanning the walls of Spearfish Canyon rising east and west of them. Hundreds of men could hide in those crags and nooks and forested ledges.

"Bad news from Stacey and Reno?" Pow asked.

Elijah nodded, his thick soup-strainer hiding the trembling in his lips. "Jimmy's in a bad way."

"How's Dotty?"

Elijah's wife, too, had come down sick with the fever only hours after Jimmy.

"She's poorly," he replied. "They all are, brother. We got nothing for them. 'Sides that, Reno and Stacey are dog tired. They can't hold up much longer if they don't get help. Damnitall anyhow, they got *nothing*!"

A third man joined them.

"Morning, gentlemen," Philly Tyler greeted them. "Any word from Fargo yet?"

"Nothing," Pow told him.

"Well, that was a dandy explosion night before last," Philly said, his moon face turned south in the direction of the Alliance Mine. "I expect great things from Fargo."

"He's only one man," Elijah reminded him.

"David was just one *boy*, yet he toppled Goliath," Philly observed before walking away.

"Since when does Philly get out of bed before noon?" Pow wondered. "He's been asking about Fargo ever since he left. What I don't get is, why ain't Philly cleared out by now and saved his own bacon? He's got no stake here, he can hustle suckers anywhere."

"I don't know," Elijah said. "All I do know is that if Jimmy and Dotty and the rest don't get help, and quick. . . ."

He didn't finish the thought, unable to face the possible loss of his wife and son.

"I figure we got a day, maybe a little longer," Pow said. "For Fargo to bring help, I mean."

Elijah scratched at his boar-bristled chin with his free hand. The other held his long Jennings rifle balanced over one shoulder. On top of all their other troubles, the Alliance thugs had released a rabid wolf in the canyon. It had already infected several of their dogs.

"I dunno about Fargo," Elijah fretted. "He's got starch in him, but it's a mighty tall order. A little over one day left. . . ."

Elijah had to pause and swallow. He was on the brink of tears.

"It ain't much time, Pow," he added. "But I got to be strong, I got to for them. If we get sick too . . . well, Fargo's all we got now. I just pray God will give him wings, or it'll be too late."

A numbing blow walloped Fargo in the back of the right thigh as the hidden marksman's bullet tagged him low of his vitals. He knew, within moments after he was hit, that it wasn't a serious wound. But he dropped flat and lay still, taking the hot pain.

"Did you two buy tickets to the show?" he demanded in a low voice when Doc Boone and Colleen just stood there open-mouthed, staring at him in shock. "Lower your skyline! That shooter's still out there."

They ducked low and scrambled into the sheltered space between the supply wagon and the buggy.

"Skye!" Colleen exclaimed. "I'm coming over there! You're hurt and bleeding."

"That bullet's a long way from my heart," he assured her. "Hurts something fierce, but I've had worse. You just stay put until I say it's safe."

"Whoever it is, he must be a humdinger of a shot," Doc remarked. "He had to be at least five hundred yards off."

Fargo lay with his ear just off the ground, knowing if he pressed it flat to earth he'd hear nothing but his own heartbeat. Soon he detected it: the faint, hollow drumbeat of a shod horse, growing fainter.

"I think he's gone for now," Fargo told the others. "But this one's tricky enough to ride in a circle just to fox us. Doc, patch me up quick."

Boone grabbed his leather medical kit from the buggy and crossed to Fargo, his niece at his side.

"The hell you think *you're* doing, young woman?" Boone demanded.

"Uncle Josh! I always assist you when—"

"Not by a jugful, missy! You'll go off behind that tree and avert your eyes. I'll have to yank this jasper's britches down, and *you* ain't getting a free peep show to put thoughts in your head. Not the way you been throwing yourself at him."

She flushed with indignation and anger. "That's just vile! The poor man—"

"Honey," Fargo cut in, wincing with pain, "just do what the old whiskey sponge says, huh? This *poor man* needs doctorin'."

Pouting, she stomped off. Doc Boone worked Fargo's trousers down and rinsed the wound off with medicinal alcohol, making Fargo twitch at the burning.

"Took a nice chunk from the back of your thigh," Boone reported. "But the slug passed through with no deep penetration. I'll flush it good. If that wound don't mortify, you'll live."

Being none too gentle about it, Doc Boone flushed the wound with more alcohol and wrapped the leg in linen bandages.

"Now here's the thing," Fargo said when Doc had finished. "Coyote, or whoever it is, could've circled back, could be watching us right now. I want him off-guard a little, so we're going to make him think I'm worse off than I am. I want the two of you to lift me into the supply wagon."

"It'll herniate me," Boone complained. "Big, strapping fellow like you! Bad 'nuff I got the bunion problem."

"Doc," Fargo said, "you're enough to vex a saint, know that? Just stop being such a contrary cuss and play along."

Struggling, with Doc Boone muttering curses, he and Colleen somehow got Fargo into the back of the wagon.

"Now I understand," Colleen remarked, "why the word travel comes from travail."

"Oh, we ain't even hit the rough stretch yet," Fargo assured her.

They set out, Doc driving the buggy, Colleen the supply wagon. Breakfast was a chunk of cold pone, eaten while they traveled. Fargo, despite the pain burning his leg, laughed out loud when Colleen took a hog-bristle toothbrush from her purse and began scrubbing her teeth.

"All the comforts of home, huh?" he teased her from the back of the wagon.

"I never know when you *might* decide to just up and kiss me," she teased back. "So I need to be ready."

The morning heated up as the sun arced higher. To

Fargo's amazement, Colleen continued to act as if they were merely on a Sunday excursion, not under constant threat of deadly fire. Not only did she shelter under a pink parasol, but she was paying more attention to the penny dreadful she was reading than to the trail ahead.

However, Fargo detected signs that danger lurked everywhere. Including occasional mirror flashes that could have been Hollis's thugs, Sioux, or both. And he still believed Coyote was out there somewhere, waiting to see if he had finished the job. Doc Boone was no immediate threat to the enemy: he could be killed at any point. It was the Trailsman Coyote had been ordered to kill.

So Fargo used the wide cracks between the boards of the supply wagon to keep a close eye out for possible clues to Coyote's whereabouts.

And eventually he got one.

They had reached Dearfield Lake, and Doc Boone and Colleen had unhitched the horses to drink. Fargo, studying the surrounding forested slopes, spotted a group of birds suddenly fly up and scatter, obviously startled off.

"I'll be back in a shake," he told the other two, dropping the tailgate and rolling out, favoring his wounded right leg.

"Where are you going?" Colleen demanded as Fargo slid his Henry from its saddle boot. "You're wounded, you should rest that leg."

"Can't. I think maybe our friend Coyote is close by, and we'd best get shed of him. I'm tired of looking over my shoulder—we got enough trouble ahead."

Colleen started to raise another protest. But Fargo, limping yet moving quickly, had already slipped into a dry wash and disappeared from sight.

Only about twelve miles north of Dearfield Lake there was an ancient, mysterious cave which extended for miles underground. The walls bristled with carvings, drawings, and inscriptions. Sioux medicine men claimed they were spirit writings as old as the *Paha Sapa* itself.

Over the years, annual delegations of Indians had visited Ghost Cave to leave offerings: decorated arrows, obsidian knives, beaded moccasins, shirts with fancy quillwork. Otherwise they avoided the place, which made it a perfect secret hideout for Cas Merrill, Boyd Lofley, and Orrin Jones. A hideout that even Mitt Brennan knew nothing about.

"Fargo's been hit!" Boyd gloated at he returned to the interior of the cave from his post outside. He carried his rifle. "I just caught the mirror signal. Coyote shot him earlier this morning."

"Kill him?" Cas demanded.

"Naw, the signal was four flashes—that means shot, not killed."

Cas shook his head. "That don't cut no ice with me. A man like Fargo don't give up the ghost easy. We seen that already with the way he escaped our pitfall and that rockslide we sent down on him."

"Yeah, but if he's still alive, that means one of *us* can still earn the two-thousand dollar bonus Hollis offered," Orrin pointed out.

Cas gave a scornful grunt. "I'll tell you the hard-cash facts, Orrin. That bonus don't amount to a hill of beans next to what we stand to profit if we play this smart."

Orrin knuckled back his campaign hat with its yellow cavalry cord, frowning. "I never bragged on being too smart. I don't catch your drift."

"What's to catch? You seen how Hollis dresses that fancy frog slut of his? Fifty-dollar gowns, mister, for a whore! Just because Mitt is willing to take crumbs from Hollis Blackburn's table don't mean *we* got to be. That Limey crumpet-muncher thinks he's a pretty high muckety-muck. But I ain't one for truckling to people of rank like Mitt does. Two-thousand dollars? Hell, that's spider leavings compared to the gold Hollis has got hid somewhere in that house of his. Gold that's minted and ready to spend. *We* take all the risk, boys! And for what?"

"For mince pie, that's what," Boyd chimed in bitterly. He had seated himself on an old packing crate and was nervously snapping one of his spur wheels. "While old Hollis lives high on the hog, even got himself a fancy hoor."

Cas nodded. "The way you say. So why don't we just ladle off some of the cream for ourselves? Kill Hollis, and Mitt if we have to, then clean out Hollis's gold stash and hightail it?"

"Deal me in," Boyd said. "Hell, this whole area is boiling with pissed-off Sioux, anyway."

"But the thing is," Cas cautioned, "none of this plan works if word ever gets out about them sick prospectors we brought into the Black Hills—we'll be hunted for life. That means we can't pull our double-cross on Hollis until *after* his strike force wipes out the prospectors who ain't killed off by fever. We can't have *no* survivors, or we'll never sleep in peace."

"Including Fargo," Boyd said.

Cas nodded. "Especially Fargo. He knows too much, and he's the kind who likes to poke his nose into the pie. We need him cold, boys—cold as a basement floor. If Coyote don't put his fire out permanent, it's up to us to finish the job."

"The trail to Busted Hump is just a whoop and a holler from here," Boyd said confidently. "He can't slip past us."

Orrin, however, looked uncertain. "I don't know about all this, boys. So much killing don't set right with me. Fargo and Hollis, sure. But Mitt? We've knowed him for years. And us helping to wipe out the camp at Busted Hump—there's women and kids there."

"The hell's got into you?" Boyd demanded. "You turning religious on us?"

"It ain't that, you idiot. But like you said, Boyd, this area's crawling with Sioux, and they're bilin' mad. Plus there could be warrants issued for our arrest. Old Hollis ruled the roost around here 'til he bucked antlers with Fargo. Now, who knows? I say let's just cut our losses and head back to the South Pass country."

"You're folding too soon," Cas insisted. "It's all coming to the grand pot now, and if we just hold on a couple more days, we can turn some dung into strawberries. As for killing Mitt, we'll give him the choice: he can side with us or feed worms with Hollis. For right now, though, let's just make sure Fargo and that damn doctor don't get past us."

Fargo had already made a mental map of the spot where he'd seen those birds startled off. Assuming Coyote would be moving forward from that spot, toward the lake, Fargo moved to intercept him.

He kept his weight on his heels to minimize chances of ground noises giving him away. He had already loosened his Colt in its holster and knocked off the riding thong. Now he levered a round into the breech of his Henry. He advanced toward his intercept point in fast bursts punctuated by pauses to look and listen. He used rocks, trees, any cover he could find.

Fargo froze when he heard a horse snorting. Gazing intently through the trees to his left, he spotted a claybank gelding hobbled foreleg to rear. But there was no sign of the rider.

He angled even farther to the right, hoping his gamble paid off. If Coyote made it to the lake first, he might decide to finish off Doc Boone and Colleen.

He hadn't even completed that thought when he heard, coming from directly behind him, the metallic click of a hammer being thumbed back. And suddenly he realized how foolishly he had underestimated this killer.

Acting on honed reflex, Fargo tucked and rolled even as the rifle barked behind him. A white-hot, razor-thin line of pain licked across his back as the bullet barely creased him.

He hit the ground, rolled hard, and came up in a kneeling off-hand position. He glimpsed Coyote's beaded shirt and dirty sailcloth trousers but had no time to notch an accurate bead. Coyote was already hammering his position again, firing a Volcanic repeating rifle.

Fargo's only cover was some low rocks. He began firing and levering, half-exposed, sending out a spray of lead to intimidate Coyote into seeking cover. But the stone-faced half-breed shouted a piercing kill cry and advanced with his rifle leaping in his hands.

Coyote had a thirty-shot magazine, Fargo realized, against seventeen rounds in the Henry. And obviously he meant to stand pat, shoot faster, and score the first hit.

It all happened in moments, but for Fargo time seemed to drag on with terrifying slowness; he steeled himself to the fact that his world might end with each second that dragged by. He was aware of the acrid stink of spent powder, the blue, filmy haze of gun smoke, the wooden stock of his Henry slapping his cheek with each shot. The rifle's ejector clicked with well-oiled smoothness, and hot shell casings rattled among the rocks.

Coyote stumbled as one of Fargo's bullets tagged his leg, but incredibly, caught himself and suddenly renewed his charge, uttering his yipping war cry as he continued to fire rapidly.

Finish it, Fargo rallied himself.

Bullets fanned his head, chunked into the rocks, tugged at the folds of his shirt and trousers. But Fargo took that extra second, aiming center of mass and squeezing the trigger back slow and easy to control bucking the rifle. His next round ripped into Coyote's chest and sent off a plume of scarlet blood. The killer went down in a sliding sprawl.

Not taking any chances with this awesome human weapon, Fargo tossed several finishing shots into the downed man.

"The vultures'll feast tonight," Fargo told the corpse. "Any man who tries to plug me can bury himself."

He went back to retrieve the claybank. Fargo wished he could feel relief. But as he headed back down toward the lake, leading the gelding, he thought about all the Alliance thugs still lurking out there to make sure he and Doc Boone never reached Busted Hump. And he remembered Kills in Water's warning from yesterday: *Once the war cry sounds, the bloodletting will begin.*

9

"Is it over, Skye?" Colleen asked in a nervous voice as Fargo limped into view leading the claybank.

"It is for Coyote," he replied as he tied the gelding to the tailgate of the supply wagon. He noticed that Doc Boone, impervious to the danger, had passed out again in the buggy. "As for the three of us," Fargo added, "I'm afraid the fandango is just beginning."

"We could all be killed, couldn't we?"

Fargo gazed into her honey-gold eyes. "Distinct possibility," he replied frankly. "That's what I warned you before we set out. But I don't plan to make it easy for 'em."

"I know you don't. And it's not fear of death that's playing on my mind, Skye. Those people at the camp have to be helped. It's just that . . . well, if we *are* killed, that means that you and I . . . well, that we never got the chance to—you know."

Fargo grinned. His eyes raked the slim length of her, from the well-turned ankles to the rich cinnamon hair. Her skin looked like creamy lotion, and a little beauty mark on her right cheek excited him for some pleasant reason.

"Well now," he replied. "Seems you got a point there."

He glanced at Doc Boone, who was sawing logs like a Minnesota lumber crew.

"Don't worry about him," Colleen urged, taking Skye's hand in hers and tugging in the direction of the thick treeline. "He killed a third of a bottle while you were gone."

"That old drunken blowhard uncle of yours ain't the problem," Fargo replied, still resisting her tugging though reluctantly. "It's *time* that's nipping at our sitters. We got maybe one full day, if we're lucky, to get to Busted Hump in time to help the sick."

"I know. But you told me it's less than fifteen miles from here."

He nodded. "Sure, and making that distance would be easier than buttering biscuits *if* we didn't have half the devils in hell trying to stop us."

"Oh, botheration!" she snapped, so vexed and frustrated that she stamped her foot. "We don't have to take too long, do we? I mean, well, I'd *love* to do it all night long with you. But even a little taste of pleasure is better than none, right? We can even leave most of our clothes on. Unless, of course, I'm not desirable enough to you? If that's the—"

Fargo silenced her by placing a finger on her lips. "You got enough mouth for an extra set of lips, know that?"

"Good. That's even more kissing."

To add to her persuasion, she ran one hand up inside his shirt, curling his chest hair around her fingers.

"You're playing with fire, m'heart," he warned her.

"Some heat doesn't burn," she assured him, rising way up on tiptoes to blow in his ear. "It just gives pleasure. Oh, I'll make it *so* good, Skye, I promise. I know I'm being shameless, but you've just got me on fire between my legs."

"That tears it for duty," he murmured, sweeping her up off her feet and carrying her toward the woods.

She started passionately kissing him even before he laid her down, her tongue exploring his mouth and darting in and out with excited hunger. Colleen let one hand dangle to stroke the hard tent in his trousers, making it doubly hard to walk but well worth the extra effort.

Fargo knelt to place her on a soft bed of spruce boughs, then stood back up to drop his trousers. He hung his gun belt from a nearby tree limb, Colt near to hand.

Colleen gazed, mesmerized, at his long, curving member, swollen so hard the tip was almost purple. Whimpering in her need, she hiked her dress up above her hips and slid her linen pantaloons off over her side-button shoes, letting them dangle on one ankle. She opened her legs invitingly wide, fully exposing the deepest, pinkest depths of her.

"Put it in me, please?" she begged, so eager her taut little caboose wriggled and squirmed. "Fill me up, Skye, all of it!"

Her bush was a silky triangle slightly darker than the hair on her head. She fumbled open her bodice and pulled down her chemise, baring a pair of luscious tits with pert little strawberry nipples perfect for sucking and nipping.

Fargo tasted those sweet berries as he bent his shaft to the perfect entry angle and flexed his buttocks hard, impaling her until their pubic mounds kissed. She cried out with near-hysterical abandon, starting to gyrate her hips in a fast rhythm with his.

"Oh, lordy, Skye, you're so big I feel like you're splitting me open! Harder, Skye, *fast*er! *Do* me, *do* me, *do* me! Deeper, darling, *deep*er!"

His busy mouth switched from pert nipple to pert nipple, licking, sucking, kissing both tits as he deep-stroked her, thrusting fast, making sure his manhood rubbed her magic nubbin, building her up to an explosive frenzy.

"Oh, Skye, you're taking me higher and higher," she moaned.

Her pleasure soon grew so intense that her every breath ended on a deep groan of bliss. She wrapped both shapely legs around Fargo and locked them way up near his shoulders, trying to get every last bit of him.

"Oh, my *stars*!" she cried hoarsely, and then she shuddered violently as she peaked, over and over, losing all control as her body thrashed and writhed under him. "Oh, you're taking me across, Skye! Faster, faster! Harder! Lord, don't *ever* stop doing that!"

Fargo, too, had finally battered down the floodgates. Pleasure had built to a hot, insistent ache in his groin, and her own release triggered his. Again and again he exploded, his repeated releases so intense that it took what felt like an eternity for him to spend himself in her.

For some minutes they both lost all track of time, lying dazed and unaware in a tangle of entwined limbs. Finally, Fargo rolled up onto one elbow.

"Now that we've done it," he teased her, "are you ready to bravely accept death?"

"Surely you jest? And miss doing *that* again? Now that I've had *you,* Skye Fargo, I want to live long enough to have you again. And again and again. Only lots longer next time, and *no* shoes. Why, you're still hard," she marveled, gripping his shaft and stroking it. "You could go again right now, you handsome stud horse."

"Mercy, girl," he begged. "You're a nurse, remember? We got lives to save, and we won't if you keep doing that. We can always play again later."

"I want that in writing," she joked as he helped her up. "Lord, now that I've had you, how will I *ever* keep my hands on top the blankets at night?"

Fargo winked. "Who says you have to? I won't tell if you don't."

Still favoring his wounded leg, Fargo led her back down to the lake.

"Wake up, Uncle Josh!" she called out. "It's time to go."

The old grump started, almost toppling out of the buggy.

"Dadgumit, girl! You scared the bejabbers out of me. Good thing you woke me, though. I was having this bad dream, there was a girl screaming out in the woods, in horrible pain."

As the sleep glaze cleared from his eyes, they narrowed in suspicion. Too late, Fargo noticed the grass clinging all over Colleen's dress and the back of her hair. They were both so dazed and drunk with pleasure they'd forgotten to brush her off.

"Where you two been?" he demanded.

"I don't answer to you or any man," Fargo told him. "As for your niece, case you haven't noticed, she's not a girl. She's a woman. She don't require your permission to live."

"Don't blow smoke up my ass, Fargo! Her being a woman is precisely the point. That's the species most in danger around a quiff hound like you."

He stared at his niece. "Fess up, girl. Where you been?"

"I ran out to see if Mr. Fargo needed medical help. While you were in a drunken stupor, he was defeating the man trying to kill us. Then we were just picking flowers for a few minutes and talking," she replied evasively.

"Picking flowers, huh? Don't hand me that guff! Where are they?"

"Didn't find any I liked."

"That's a lulu!" He stared at Fargo, so angry even his bald dome flushed red. "Picking cherries is more like it, eh, Fargo?"

You'll shake no cherries off *that* fine bush, Fargo mused, but wisely kept the thought to himself.

"Never mind, you old mash vat," Fargo told him. "You brace me once more with that pepperbox and I'll knock you into next week, that's a promise. We got far bigger problems than your blue-nosed ranting. You pull the cork one more time between here and Busted Hump, I'm pouring out your joy juice. I want you sober when we get there."

"Sober? Fargo, I can't practice medicine sober, I don't know how! And pour out my liquor?" Boone looked scared for the first time since Fargo had met him. "Anything but that, please!"

"All right then, get that buggy hitched," he ordered. "From here on out, we're up against it bad. Both of you keep a weather eye out, and don't lose your head if trouble comes. Because believe me, it will."

Fargo led them due north on a course to intersect with Spearfish Creek. The next few miles were rocky and rough, and recent rains made muddy bottoms that mired the wagon. Twice Fargo had to untie the Ovaro and the claybank and use their extra pulling power to get the vehicle unstuck. The hard labor was bad enough. But he especially resented the loss of precious time.

As if they didn't have troubles enough, before long he could hear the rear axle squealing. He tried to ignore it. Before long, however, the sound became a steady screeching.

Cussing the old man back in Busted Hump for his laziness, he reined in and first took a good look around. The forested mountains rose all around them, dark even in the morning sunlight.

"What the hell's wrong now?" Doc Boone complained, reining in beside him. "Or are you just enjoying the view?"

"Keep pushing, old man," Fargo muttered as he climbed down. "I swear, I'll gag that mouth of yours yet."

"At least let me have a nip while you're wasting time."

"Nip? I wouldn't give you the sweat off my . . ." Fargo glanced over at Colleen. "Off my hat band," he finished.

Wincing at the pain in his leg, Fargo crawled under the conveyance and greased the axle from a bucket that hung underneath.

Despite Fargo's orders, Doc Boone nodded out again during the delay. Suddenly his horse farted loudly, and the old man woke up with a start.

"Did an angel speak?" he muttered.

"Stick a sock in it and get rolling," Fargo told him, climbing into the wagon again and taking up the reins.

Another slow mile passed, Fargo's eyes constantly scanning to all sides. It bothered him that a brisk tail wind blew—the Ovaro had an acute sense of smell, but it was worthless now because all the danger lay ahead of them, upwind.

At a wide spot in the trail, Doc Boone brought his buggy alongside Fargo. "Can't I have just a nip to wash my teeth?" he whined again. "This ain't Christian of you, Fargo."

Fargo opened his mouth to answer, but the words snagged in his throat. Up ahead, at least a dozen mounted, well-armed Sioux braves had just debouched from the trees and taken up a line across the trail.

"Tender Virgin!" Doc Boone exclaimed. His eyes bulged out like a squashed toad's.

Colleen turned pale and went wide-eyed with fright. "Skye! Oh my lord, Skye, what—?"

"Stay calm," he urged both of them quietly. "The last thing you want to do is show them you're scared. Keep your fear out of your face. A Sioux despises a coward."

Despite his own calm manner, however, Fargo felt a little cool sweat break out in his armpits. He knew this was going to get ugly. Those braves were painted and wore their coup feathers—which meant they had purified themselves for battle and could now kill in the *Paha Sapa* without angering their gods. Kills in Water had warned him of a massed strike soon, one to include all seven bands of the Lakota. But Fargo hadn't expected trouble this quickly.

"Leave it lay," he snapped when Doc Boone reached for the pepperbox on the seat beside him. "Those aren't your usual drunk miners in town, Doc. Those are battle-hardened warriors. We ain't shooting our way out of this one."

Four of the braves walked their horses forward. Two held old British trading rifles aimed at their new prisoners. The other two were armed with strong bows, arrows with flaked-flint points already notched. One of them rode closer and snatched Fargo's Colt out of its holster.

A fierce-looking brave with eyes like black agates began shouting at Fargo in the Lakota tongue.

"Fargo," Doc said, his voice tight with fear, "I only pala-ver two languages, American and cussing. The hell's he saying?"

"I caught the word *itanchan*, he's saying he's a big chief. From what I savvy of the rest of it, Doc, you don't want to know."

"That bad?"

"Worse. This tough-looking buck is named Winter Bear. I'm guessing he's their clan leader. Sounds like we have to go back to their camp with them. It's an order, not an invitation."

Hearing these words, Colleen appeared to be on the verge of swooning from fright.

"Nerve up!" Fargo snapped at her. "You, too, Doc. Get that fear off your faces *now*. The only chance we got is to be defiant and show some guts. A Sioux is a notional creature. If they decide we've got courage, we just *might* wangle out of this with our dander intact. I've done it before."

Winter Bear, the apparent leader, shouted something and the rest of his braves rode forward. The whiteskins were dragged from their vehicles. Colleen resisted, screaming and kicking. Then Fargo saw her pull the buggy whip out of its socket.

"Colleen, *no*, you little fool!" he snapped at her. "I said defiant, not crazy!"

But he was too late. She lashed a brave across the face. Enraged, he slammed the muzzle of his rifle into the side of her head, and she slumped unconscious.

"You piece of red trash!" Doc Boone exclaimed, lunging toward the brave. Fargo caught him by the collar and hauled him back.

"Ease off, you old fool," he ordered the fuming doctor. "That was just a love tap compared to what she could have got."

Two braves unhitched the team horses while another untied the Ovaro and Coyote's claybank. Fargo and Doc Boone, weapons constantly trained on them, were ordered to mount the two saddle horses. Fargo's Arkansas Toothpick was yanked from its boot sheath. Two braves tossed Colleen roughly up onto Fargo's saddle, and he held her with one arm. She was still breathing and already coming around.

Doc Boone's ginger, a good horse only about six years old, was then tied to a lead line. But after a brief discussion, both worn-out team horses were shot in the head.

There goes the supply delivery, Fargo thought. And if they get into that medicine, it's all over for the sick folks at Busted Hump. But then again, it hardly appeared as if any of them would survive to complete the mercy mission anyway.

One brave had already taken Fargo's Henry from its saddle boot. When they realized the wagon was filled with valuable goods, including powder and lead, they quickly pushed it into the trees, obviously intending to come back for the supplies.

"Oh, Jesus," Fargo muttered when one of the braves found Doc Boone's old pepperbox pistol on the seat of the buggy.

Unable to recall the Lakota word for danger, Fargo made the sign for it, a clenched fist striking his heart.

"Careful with that!" he shouted. But several more quarreling braves had gathered around their comrade who was holding this curious-looking weapon. Fargo winced as they fought over it, one grabbing it from the other. All of them ignored his warnings. Abruptly, Miss Pepper exploded with a deafening roar, all six barrels firing.

Winter Bear's fine-looking piebald stallion caught all six bullets and dropped like a stone beneath him. The clan leader barely got his legs up in time to avoid being pinned when the horse collapsed. Blood spurted from its flank with an obscene splashing noise.

"*That* caps the climax," Fargo muttered to Doc Boone. "That piebald was his best battle horse—see all the red hand prints painted on it? Each one marks a coup in battle on that stallion."

His eyes smoky with rage, Winter Bear glowered at the whiteskin prisoners. He grabbed the pepperbox, slapped the brave who had mistakenly fired it, then flung the weapon off into the underbrush.

Winter Bear swung up behind another brave and shouted an order. With armed Sioux behind them, Fargo and Doc Boone followed as the braves veered off the trail and headed up the slope, threading their way through spruce and pine trees. Winter Bear's anger was palpable and had spread to the rest of his braves.

"What happens now?" Doc Boone asked Fargo.

"Might's well ask me what comes after what's next," Fargo replied. "I ain't found no way yet to read sign when it comes to figuring out the red man's way of thinking. Likely, they feel the same about us whites."

Fargo tightened his grip on Colleen. "But I can tell you this much, you canon-toting old fool: There ain't *nothing* a Sioux warrior values more than his prize war horse. I should have took that old pepperbox of yours away from you in Shoshone Falls and stuck it where the sun don't shine. Now we'll all be damn lucky if our scalps don't end up dangling from a totem pole."

"Mitt, you and I need to have a little talk," Hollis Blackburn told his mine captain. "Certain facts must be faced squarely. Our situation here in the Black Hills has always been precarious. But events are now threatening to overtake us."

The Alliance Mine was such a major operation that it had even developed its own mercury mine on site, mercury being required for the reduction of gold. It was in front of this open-pit mine that the two men met about midmorning.

"What events?" Mitt Brennan asked. "Fargo, you mean?"

Hollis shook his head, smiling smugly. "I said *events*, Mitt. Fargo is only a man, and one man will never stop Hollis Blackburn. He's either already dead or soon will be. No, the problem I mean is the Sioux. I made attempts recently to placate their leaders. But those unprincipled savages accepted my trade goods, then broke their promise. I've received a reliable new report. They've been fasting and purifying themselves at Bear Butte just east of here. Now they're greased for war and filtering back into the Black Hills, preparing to strike. It will be open season on whiteskins."

Mitt whistled. "I knew it was bad down in the Platte Valley. How soon before they hit?"

"Any time now," Hollis replied. "Which is why I've made arrangements, at some considerable expense, to rendezvous with a flatboat. The Belle Fourche River skirts the Black Hills just past their northeastern tip—we can make it to Bridger's Landing in six hours. Once I flash the signal, that boat will be waiting."

Mitt's long jaw fell open in astonishment. "Hell, the mine's going flat out, Mr. Blackburn. Right now as we speak, the mining engineer is dropping plumb lines to explore new shafts. Not to mention all that color sitting just underneath the camp at Busted Hump."

As if to underscore Mitt's point, they could feel, through the soles of their boots, the rumble of ore cars on narrow-gauge tracks below ground.

Mitt went on: "This is no time to desert those stopes. The water table here is close to the surface. They'll fill up with water, and—"

"Gold is useless to dead men, Mitt. Which is what you and I will both be if we don't pull foot soon."

Mitt rubbed his chin, looking troubled and uncertain. "Hard to argue with logic like that. But what about your contract with the owners of the Alliance?"

Hollis shrugged, picking a piece of lint off the sleeve of his tailored tweed suitcoat. It was too late now to mine any more ore in the Black Hills, and it wasn't his problem what happened to those too stupid to realize it. He and Suzette had begun making plans to slip away with a tidy profit. As Mine Supervisor, he had plenty of minted gold at his disposal for purchasing supplies and equipment. Since he needed a man to help him cart all the gold he planned to steal, and protect him en route, he needed to bring Mitt in on it. Once the escape was completed, he would simply shoot Brennan—Blackburn's legal training had taught him never to leave witnesses to his crimes.

"And what about the miners?" Mitt added. "Most of them got no transportation. They know nothing about this Sioux uprising. How—?"

"As the poet says," Hollis interrupted. " 'The sweetest meat sticks to my own bones.' Mitt, these miners aren't children, they chose to come into these dangerous hills. I wish them no ill, but *we* have a chance to live, Mitt, to enjoy riches and a good life. We'd be fools to die in some useless attempt to save the others."

"Would Cas, Orrin, and Boyd be getting out with us?"

"Don't be a simp! Trust *those* three with all that gold tempting them? You I trust. But not them. Talk about leaving foxes in charge of the hen house."

Again Mitt pulled at his chin, pox-scarred face troubled. "I ain't too keen on the idea of just leaving them in the lurch. I rode with them for years."

Hollis gave a scornful bark of laughter. "Those jackals? Believe me, Mitt, they know which way the wind sets. They're making *their* plans, too, count upon it. And don't be naive enough to believe those plans include you. They see you as my minion."

"Minion?" Mitt repeated. "Can't say as I know that word."

You ignorant American blockhead, Hollis thought. Out loud he said patiently: "It means they see you as loyal to me, not them."

Mitt slowly nodded. Hollis had always been a persuasive

man. "Could be you're right. I notice they have been keeping to themselves more."

His face brightened for a moment as something else occurred to him. "Since we'll be hightailing it, does that mean we can forget about the raid on the prospectors at Busted Hump? Sounds like the Sioux will wipe them out for us."

Hollis shook his head emphatically. "We must paddle our own canoe. We can't risk relying on Sioux or plague to finish off those prospectors. Not after Orrin and Boyd made that stupid, *stupid* move of actually bringing sick prospectors here and then just dumping them to die where Fargo could find them. If we wipe that camp out, and cleverly blame it on the Sioux, Fargo won't have any proof to back a court action."

Mitt turned the problem back and forth for a while. He found Hollis convincing, but he had worked off and on with the other three men for many years now.

Hollis, meantime, was smiling in his thoughts. He never left anything to chance. He had expected Mitt to hang fire on this matter, so he'd taken steps to bring in more persuasive measures.

And she was sashaying toward the two men right now, bringing them a picnic basket and a bottle of wine. Like most men in this woman-scarce camp, Mitt lusted for Suzette. Following Hollis's orders, she made sure to show up this morning "just by chance."

"Bonjour," she called out, flashing a gay, flirtatious smile at Mitt. She lifted a dainty little lace napkin covering the basket. "I have bring you two hard-working mens san'-weeches and blueberries pie."

Mitt stared, for she wore a boldly revealing velvet damask dress with a plunging bodice. Tight corset lacings thrust her breasts out like ripe, succulent fruits ready to be plucked.

"Suzette specifically requested that you be our guard, Mitt, when we make our hasty exit."

She batted long, curving lashes at the mine captain. "Some nights, Hollis must be gone on ze business matters, *non*? I need a strong man to stay with me and protect me."

Hollis grinned when Mitt flushed. "Come, come, Mitt, we're both men of the world. Nobody misses a slice off a cut loaf. I can't keep this pretty little demon satisfied by myself anyway—she has the carnal appetite of a Cleopatra."

"You don't say?" Mitt stared at Suzette, who preened for him.

"And your gun, Mitt," she cooed, stroking the butt of his Smith & Wesson. "Such a manly and fright-en-ing weapon! My Hollis, he has ze courage. But his gun, you see it there? A toy!"

"Speaking of that," Mitt remarked to his boss, "I've noticed that you've taken to wearing that fancy-carved Swiss gun of yours. Use to, you kept it to home."

"It's Belgian, not Swiss," Hollis corrected him. "A fine Belgian pinfire. And I think we've already covered the reasons why I'm wearing it."

"Is it true that thing fires paper cartridges?"

"Yes, but believe me, the bullets aren't paper."

Suzette put one ivory-white, perfectly manicured hand on Mitt's arm. "You are so much ze rugged type. I hope you go with us."

"What do you say, Mitt?" Hollis pressed him. "Those three associates of yours are just worthless yahoos anyway. It was *their* stupidity that alerted Fargo in the first place. It's going to be every man for himself and the devil take the hindmost. You have a right to save your own hide. Are you with us?"

Suzette's hand stroked Mitt's arm. "Pleez, Mitt? I will feel *so* much safe."

"Deal me in," Mitt decided, his voice a little husky.

A satisfied smile spread under Hollis's neatly hirsute upper lip.

"Good man! But first things first, stout lad. While we wait to hear final word on Fargo, you keep organizing that strike force. At least forty men, all the crack shots we have. Pay them well to salve their consciences."

Hollis gazed off toward the hazy, cloud-covered peaks surrounding them. "We must leave *nothing* to chance, Mitt. We'll hit Busted Hump hard, we'll hit fast, we'll have the element of complete surprise. The same way the Royal Navy defeated the Spanish Armada. When we leave the Black Hills, there must be no incriminating evidence left behind."

10

The Sioux camp was at a high elevation but not far from the trail. For perhaps twenty minutes they ascended the mountain slope, up to where the trees started to thin, then higher still to the shadowed stone near the summit.

Colleen had regained consciousness, a huge bruise swelling over her left temple.

"You all right?" Fargo asked her.

"I guess so except for a headache. Skye, where are they taking us?" she asked in a hushed, fearful tone.

"Wherever they have a mind to," he assured her. "You just remember *not* to strike out at them again."

"But you told me not to show fear—"

"Sure. But being brave ain't the same as being stupid," he said. "An Indian brave isn't raised to tolerate a woman beating on him. To him that's not courage, it's an insult. You try that again, it could get you killed."

"We'll all be killed anyhow, damn you, Fargo," Doc Boone said behind them. "You ain't got the good sense God gave a pissant! You and your blasted 'mercy mission.'"

"You did it for the gold, greedy guts, not mercy," Fargo reminded him. "And we're not dead yet, so put some stiff in your spine. For a man who spent his life as an army doctor, you sure act like a green-antlered tenderfoot."

They reached a small, rock-strewn clearing. Fargo saw right away it was a temporary war camp—no women or children with this band, apparently, only blooded warriors. Instead of the usual elaborate tipis with hide covers, there were only crude brush wickiups for shelter.

He noticed a few stolen army mules with the U.S. brand on their hips. Probably kept for food, Fargo guessed, since the braves had no time now for hunting.

He followed orders and dismounted, then helped Colleen

down. She was still woozy from the blow, and he sat her down with her back to a pine tree.

Perhaps another dozen braves had been waiting here in the camp. Now they all gathered round in a circle, staring at the captives. Several seemed especially fascinated by Colleen's flawless, creamy white skin. One snatched off Doc Boone's derby and pointed at the white man's bald dome. He said something and the rest howled with mirth.

"The hell's so funny?" Doc fumed, irritated despite his fear.

"He's joking about how you ain't worth scalping," Fargo explained.

"*That's* good news, at least," Boone replied.

"Not hardly. If a brave can't take your scalp, he'll maybe peel off the facial skin to verify his kill. Or remove your scrotum and tan it for a pouch."

"*Remove* the scrotum? . . ."

Doc Boone turned a sickly green as he pictured that. Fargo, glancing around, noticed a ground sheet spread out in the middle of the clearing. It was piled high with trade goods: knives, bolts of red strouding, mirrors, beads, even a coffee grinder.

Winter Bear saw Fargo studying the pile. The war leader shouted a name, and now Fargo saw the group did indeed include at least one female. She came quickly forward. He saw she was white, so he guessed why they'd brought her along for their battle campaign: she must be their translator, perhaps a captive who had gone over to the Sioux way of life.

Winter Bear pointed at the goods and said something in a scornful tone. A few braves laughed. The woman, dressed in white buckskin with fancy quillwork, translated.

"You are looking at 'valuable' gifts from the Englishman. Most of it useless women's trinkets. There was some tobacco, but dry and bitter. No whiskey or guns. Could it possibly be that he fears us ignorant savages?"

Hollis Blackburn again, Fargo thought. Working behind the scenes and stirring up trouble. That's one man I surely plan to meet.

But now Winter Bear, who was on his dignity as leader, had jumped up onto a tree stump to speak. The old woman translated.

"The *Paha Sapa* belongs to the Lakota people, and we do not welcome *any* of you whiteskins. The first great liar among you was Sharp Knife, whom your people call Andrew Jackson. He promised if the red man moved west of the Great Waters all that land would be ours. Then the yellow rocks were found in the *Paha Sapa*, and once again you expect the red man to strike his lodges and go where you whiteskins send him—into worthless places no white man wants. Your chiefs speak from both sides of their mouths."

"I speak one way always," Fargo assured him through the translator. "Your complaint is just. But it is not only the red men who are cheated by these lying chiefs. These powerful miners and railroad men destroy anyone or anything that gets in their path. They destroy poor whites to take their land and homes. Honor means nothing to them, only riches."

Winter Bear scowled, his stern features heavy with contempt. "You speak like the general named Harney. He, too, pretended sympathy for us. We foolishly listened to his lies. He promised us things his chiefs in Washington city refused to pay for. Our old men, too stiff to wage battle, have already given white men too much of our land. But this *Paha Sapa*, *never* can we surrender this."

Winter Bear spread both arms wide. Copper brassards encircled them, protection during battle.

"It is here," he resumed through the translator, "through a secret hole, in a cave known only to a few medicine men, that We-Ota-Wichasa, Blood Clot Man, came up to live on earth and make First People. The white man cannot write up papers to claim land as his, for the land owns *us*. We were here before you, hair face. You should have gone digging for glittering rocks elsewhere."

"I ain't here to dig anything," Fargo replied. "And I meant to swing wide of the *Paha Sapa*. But two of your young bucks stole my horse. You can't leave a man afoot in open country, you know that. I came for my horse and I got him. Now, as soon as you clear my trail, I mean to leave."

Many braves seemed amused by Fargo's calm manner and foolish statements about leaving—as if *he* were in charge.

"You say two of my young bucks took your horse?" Winter Bear said. "Point them out to me."

Fargo studied the hostile faces ringing him. "I don't see 'em. They're younger than these men anyway. They must be with another band."

Hoots of derision followed Fargo's remark

"Perhaps it is true," Winter Bear said, taking a long look at Doc Boone and Colleen, "that you three are not gold-seekers. You, hair face, look like a warrior. And this pretty girl and this fat, worthless old man with the smooth head—they are too soft for this country. Why are you still here if you have your horse back?"

"Fat?" Doc Boone muttered so only Fargo and Colleen heard him. "Kiss my ass, you double-poxed hound."

Fargo explained the situation with mountain fever at Busted Hump and introduced Doc Boone as a *wichasa wakan* or medicine man.

"We are only trying to save lives," he concluded. "Not take anything from the red man."

"Yes, but you save the wrong lives," Winter Bear insisted. "You save those who have invaded our sacred mountains. So you will die along with those who defile our holy ground."

Fargo saw things were going to hell quick. He was gaining nothing by being defensive. So he rolled the dice and decided to stand up to this brave with a more aggressive defense.

"Stretching the blanket a mite, ain't you? Those prospectors didn't come here to hurt you," he told the Sioux leader. "You act so high and mighty, like the red man does no wrong, only the white man. But I've watched your people drive an entire buffalo herd over a cliff just to eat a few of them. I've watched red men chop down a whole tree just to get a few nuts at the top. I've seen you make a public entertainment out of torturing women. *No* people are perfect, yours included."

His remarks made Winter Bear's scowl etch itself deeper. Again he spoke through the woman translator.

"Hair face, I will grant this: You are no mealy-mouthed coward like most we capture. Perhaps, if my best horse had not been killed, you three would be on your way even now.

But my horse is dead. Now there must be a settling of this debt."

"We didn't kill it," Fargo reminded him.

"True. If you had, all three of you would be dying now."

Winter Bear turned to look down at Colleen. "*After* watching all my bucks mount this one and bull her. However—it was my man who shot the horse. Yet, it was *you*"—he looked right at Fargo now—"who brought the bad-medicine gun into our country. I see you, too, have a fine horse. A strong Ovaro. Now you will watch while I throat-slash this fine mount."

There was a bone-handle knife in Winter Bear's beaded sheath, sharpened only on one edge, Indian fashion. He pulled it out and advanced toward the Ovaro.

Fargo forced himself to a quick decision. He decided to gamble on the Plains warrior's respect for brazen effrontery in the face of great odds.

"This news surprises me," he said through the translator. "The last time I sneaked into your lodge and enjoyed your wife, Winter Bear, she said you were a timid fellow, afraid to make the hard thrusts."

Doc Boone and Colleen, hearing Fargo's English version, looked at him as if he must be crazy. For the Sioux, however, this was so outrageous and entertaining that it surpassed insult and became a show of admirable valor. Besides which, many caught the pun and found it a good one. Even Winter Bear, as he turned around, was so impressed that he had to make an effort to hold his face stern.

"Now, of course, you have challenged me. A fight, just the two of us. If you win, you keep your life *and* your horse. I will choose the method of combat. Agreed?"

Fargo nodded. "Let's get 'er done."

Fargo expected a knife fight with their left wrists bound together, a typical Indian version of the duel. But Winter Bear shouted out instructions: One brave ran to stir up the coals of that morning's cooking fire, fanning them until they glowed red-orange. Another brave went to fetch a long, strong rope braided from horse hair.

So it was going to be a tug-of-war over hot coals, Fargo realized. This way, the loser also became a coward if he let go of the rope before being pulled into the embers.

Winter Bear removed his triple-soled moccasins, Fargo his boots. When Winter Bear peeled off his elkskin shirt, Fargo realized why he had chosen the rope. The brave was more solidly muscled than most of the typically slender-limbed Sioux males. He was built more like the Apaches to the Southwest, with a thick chest and well-muscled arms and shoulders.

Fargo, too, stripped off his shirt. Winter Bear tossed him one end of the rope across the fire in its circle of stones. Fargo wrapped it around his hands. Both men squared off, dug in their bare heels, and waited for the signal.

Someone loosed a piercing whistle, and Winter Bear instantly gave a mighty tug. Despite being braced and ready, Fargo felt his wounded thigh momentarily give under him. He lost his balance and stumbled a few steps forward. A shout of encouragement went up from the other braves as their champion seemed on the verge of a quick victory.

But Fargo, with a supreme effort of muscle and will and balance, managed to halt his slide just before he reached the circle of stones. Loop by slow loop, he wrested more and more rope away from Winter Bear, dragging the Sioux closer to the fire.

For perhaps five minutes they strained and heaved and grunted. One moment Fargo was on the verge of winning, the next it was Winter Bear. Each man's sweat-glistening muscles stood out like taut cables.

Fargo sensed his opponent tiring. He gathered his last reserves of strength, gave a mighty pull, and Winter Bear lost his footing.

The Sioux could have let go of the rope, losing face in front of his braves but saving himself from horrible burns. Instead, he was fully prepared to land face first and bare-chested in those glowing coals. At the last second, however, several of his men reached out to catch him.

"You have beaten me fairly, hair face," the woman translated his words. "I gave my word. Take your fine horse and go. If you are as smart as you are strong, you will forget about the sick gold seekers and leave the *Paha Sapa* at once."

"Fargo, you *did* it!" exclaimed a relieved Doc Boone. "Christ, I like to died when that first tug almost sent you ass-over-applecart. But you *did* it, boy!"

This was the first and only civil remark he'd ever made to Fargo. However, when Boone started to rise from the ground, a brave shoved him back down.

"*You* may go," Winter Bear told Fargo. "I said nothing of these two."

"If they stay, I stay."

Winter Bear's face hardened, the intense, black agate eyes blazing. "As you wish. Then you will die with them also."

A shout from downslope turned all heads. Fargo felt a jolt of surprise when he recognized Kills in Water, the brave who had warned him during his ride to Shoshone Falls. But Fargo's surprise was even greater when he recognized the two youths riding with Kills in Water: the same two who had stolen Fargo's Ovaro several days ago.

The warm greeting from Winter Bear and his warriors heartened Fargo. Kills in Water rode with Spotted Tail's band, and clearly the two groups were close allies. The woman translated for the prisoners.

"Brothers!" Kills in Water greeted them all, remaining mounted to command their attention. "You know these two tadpoles with me. My youngest brother, Smiles Plenty, and his friend Panther. They ask permission to speak before warriors."

"We have ears," Winter Bear replied, staring at the boys. "But speak quickly and leave—this is no place for children. Go join the girls in their sewing lodge."

The warriors hooted and laughed, for it was the custom to constantly humiliate a young man who had not yet achieved distinction in battle or during the hunt. Neither of these two lads had yet earned his first coup feather. And they were painfully aware of that fact.

Nonetheless, both youths came forward. They told the story, taking turns, of how they managed to steal this tall hair face's fine stallion while he was afoot hunting game. But they also described how he cleverly took back his horse, yet respected the laws of the *Paha Sapa*.

"That one," Smiles Plenty said, pointing at Fargo. "He could have killed us. But he told us he would avoid shedding blood in the *Paha Sapa* except to defend his life."

The assembled braves looked at Fargo with new respect.

So did Winter Bear. It was rare for white men to even know the sacred rules of this place, much less respect them.

"I heard something about this days ago," the battle leader said. "So it was you? You could have told us this thing, when we captured you. Yet you did not. Why?"

Fargo nodded toward Doc Boone and Colleen. "Because you might have let me go. And those two are my responsibility. I knew you were going to have some sport, so I figured it should be with the man in charge."

Fargo pointed at Doc Boone. "You think *that* tub of guts is any use in a scrape? Hell, the woman with him is a better fighter."

Winter Bear nodded, understanding. "You stayed quiet to protect the weak. Now I see better the manner of man you are, Fargo. Know this. I lead only this one band, and you know there are more Lakota in the *Paha Sapa*. Seven bands in all. I cannot stay their hands, but all three of you are safe from my warriors.

"Go, then, save these people in Spearfish Canyon if you are so set on it. But if you are wise, you will warn them: Get away from here quickly!"

"Winter Bear agrees with me," Kills in Water took over, speaking in English directly to Fargo. "It is the Vulture God who most needs killing. This Hollis Blackburn, this friend to all carrion birds. Winter Bear knows, as do I, that you may become a powerful weapon in the hunt to kill him. Perhaps even the weapon that stops him."

"So that's why you bothered to warn me yesterday," Fargo said, grinning at Kills in Water. "It was your kid brother who tried to heist my stallion. Well, as to killing Hollis . . . if I get solid proof that he caused fever to be brought here, believe me, he's paying for it."

But for right now Fargo was more worried about the slant of the sun. Morning had become afternoon, and there was now less than one day to reach Busted Hump—much less than one day.

11

To show his newfound respect for Skye Fargo, Winter Bear ordered the return of Fargo's Ovaro and weapons. He also told his braves not to disturb those supplies in the wagon. And despite the loss of his favorite war mount, the Sioux leader even returned Doc Boone's horse and the strong young claybank gelding Fargo had acquired after killing Coyote.

"But we got us a real stumper of a problem," Fargo explained as the trio made their way back down to the trail. "Those two team horses they killed. They were broken to the harness. Your ginger is our only tug horse now, and we'll need it to pull your buggy."

"But then how will you haul the supplies?" Colleen asked. She rode behind Fargo, holding on so tightly to him that Doc Boone kept scowling at her.

"What I'd like to do," he replied, "is just leave that supply wagon for now and ride with you two, at least get that medicine to Busted Hump before it's too late. But even if Winter Bear and his bunch leave the supplies alone, some other band will claim them. So we've got to haul them with us."

"Why?" Doc Boone demanded. "It's the medicine they need most."

"Sure. But what's the use of saving them from fever just so they can starve?"

"All right, then. How?" Doc Boone persisted in a surly tone. He was stone-cold sober, thanks to Fargo's seizing his whiskey, and in a foul mood about it. Nor did he appreciate being forced to ride the ginger bareback—his testicles were taking a beating on the rough slope.

"Wait, don't tell me how," he added. "Skye Fargo, great Indian deity that he is, will just *miracle* those supplies into motion. Make 'em fly through the air like the great thunderbird."

"Put a stop on your gob, you grumpy old coot," Fargo snapped. "I won't swallow your bunk like your niece has to. You and that damn old pepperbox of yours—I *told* you it had a worn sear and was dangerous. A damned rented mule has got more good sense than you've got."

"I don't give a hang what you told me, Fargo, nor about what you think. And you listen to me, Colleen! Put some daylight between you and that jasper! You hold him any tighter, you'll throw off friction sparks."

"Oh, poof," she told her uncle. Then, to Fargo: "How *will* you get those supplies to the prospectors' camp, Skye?"

"Hate to say it," he replied, "but you're now riding on one half of the solution. This claybank we're leading is the other half."

"Horse apples!" Doc Boone scoffed. "Unless both animals are harness broke."

"Mine sure ain't," Fargo replied. "And I doubt the claybank has ever been fit with traces, either. But it *can* be done by wit and wile."

"*Wiles* you've got plenty of," Doc retorted. "Wits, I ain't so sure."

They reached the trail and the abandoned conveyances. Fortunately, Doc Boone's supply of laudanum and diluted carbolic was still safe, as were the supplies. Fargo's first, unpleasant task was to free those two dead horses from the hopelessly tangled traces.

Then came the even tougher part—getting the Ovaro and the claybank to submit to the harness. From Fargo's perspective, it would have been easier to put socks on a rooster.

The Ovaro clearly didn't like it, but his trust in his human master eventually allowed Fargo to buckle the stallion in. The claybank, however, hadn't even gotten used to Fargo's smell yet. It fought like a wolverine being forced to accept a collar and leash.

Fargo's only choice was bribery. Each time the hungry gelding showed signs of cooperating, Fargo fed him some oats from his hat. Eventually, the sweat-soaked, exhausted Fargo had some semblance of a team.

Until, that is, he climbed onto the board seat and snapped the reins. His Ovaro reluctantly started to pull, but the claybank whickered in anger and tried to rear up.

"Hah! So much for your brilliant plan, Fargo!" Doc

Boone mocked him. "You'd have better luck herding cats. Too bad that horse ain't a woman—*they* eat out of your hand, no doubt," he added, slanting a petulant glance toward his niece.

Fargo eventually got the reluctant horse underway. And after a half hour or so the claybank had settled down. Now Fargo's greatest concern was to constantly scan the surrounding terrain, watching for the ever-expected attack.

Soon, however, another calamity beset them. The rough terrain caused the iron tire encircling the right rear wheel to loosen. Fargo could hear it grating and thumping. He knew the proper way to fix it was to drive a wedge between the tire and the felloe. But he had no tools, so he stoically drove on, hoping the wagon would somehow limp the remaining distance.

Spearfish Creek was finally in view ahead—the last leg of the journey lay before them. Only about five miles now to Busted Hump. But Fargo feared this last stretch of trail would be more dangerous than the entire journey so far.

Busy studying the surrounding slopes, his mind occupied, he failed to swing wide of a sudden dip in the trail. The wagon bottomed out hard, lurched, and the iron tire sprang off. The unprotected wheel split on a boulder and the wagon collapsed, spilling kegs and boxes of supplies.

"Whoa!" Doc Boone shouted behind him, halting the buggy. "*Now* you've done it, Fargo! Hell, a blind hog could have avoided that hole! And they call *you* the Trailsman? I guess that makes me Davy Crockett!"

"You keep roweling me, you old goat," he warned Boone, "and that hole will be the start of a fresh grave."

He swung down and walked back to survey the damage.

"What now?" Colleen lamented. "You leave the wagon and come with us?"

Fargo shook his head, removing his hat to slap the dust from it. He studied the land all around them.

"If we leave it," he replied, "those supplies will be destroyed or stolen. That happens, it might not matter if we're on time—the prospectors could die anyway."

"You said all that before. But you can't have your cake and eat it, too," Doc Boone complained. "Either you leave the busted wagon or you stay and guard the supplies."

Fargo shook his head. "You're wrong again, as usual.

Don't forget that three of those four wheels still roll. I'm going to lash on a drag pole. Sort of a crutch for a conveyance. You two quick get the wagon unloaded."

"I need a drink first," Doc Boone carped.

"You can have a short jolt when it's finished," Fargo promised, figuring that if bribery worked on the claybank it would also work on Boone. And indeed, the old grump rolled up his sleeves and went to work like a lusty young laborer.

While Fargo searched for a thin, strong branch or sapling, the other two emptied the bed of the wagon. Fargo found his sapling, sawed it down and trimmed it with his Arkansas Toothpick, then returned to the wagon.

With Fargo's strong back bent to hold up the wagon, Doc and Colleen followed his orders and lashed the pole to the end of the axle and the sideboards, so it slanted down and kept the axle itself from dragging on the ground, acting as an unwanted brake.

"It'll pull slower and harder," Fargo conceded. He was drenched in sweat from his efforts, and now the stiff breeze felt uncomfortably cool. "But at least it'll pull. C'mon— this is more time lost and we're burning good daylight."

He was distracted for a few moments as the claybank, grown restless at the delay, tried to pull against the traces. Fargo patted the gelding's neck and spoke to it calmly, gentling the animal. But as he climbed up onto the board seat and took up the reins again, he felt his scalp tingle and tighten.

He slid the thong off his Colt and got his nerves steady for whatever was coming.

Well north of Dearfield Lake, Cas Merrill stood in the entrance to Ghost Cave and shook his head in amazement.

"The signal's been flashed: Fargo killed Coyote. I swear, boys, that man comes at you like the Apocalypse," he said with grudging admiration.

Well below him, on the rocky canyon floor approaching the creek, Skye Fargo had just finished the damndest repair job Cas had ever seen. For a man dressed in old buckskins, Fargo appeared to be a handy fellow. Dangerously handy.

"What's the Apocalypse?" Boyd Lofley called from inside the cave, where he was busy soaping his saddle.

"Never mind," Cas told him, still watching Fargo. "They're moving again. Grab your rifles and get into position. Won't be long, we'll have a plumb-perfect bead on that son of a bitch. Even if you two weak sisters miss, old Cas will split open his skullpan with this herd leveler."

He meant the Big Fifty in his hands, reserved for just such occasions. In truth, Cas knew that Boyd and Orrin were both passable shots. But he had the range advantage and intended to fire the first shot.

"This is our Adobe Walls battle, boys," he added. "With Coyote cold, it's come down to the nut-cuttin'. Neither Fargo or that sawbones gets past us. That means worry most about planting Fargo—the old man is dog meat without him anyhow. If we don't stop Fargo right now . . . hell, if we don't *kill* him right now, all our big plans are just smoke behind us."

"Speaking of plans," Orrin said as he slid his New Haven Arms repeating rifle into its buckskin sheath. "You talk to Mitt yet, give him his choices? Side with us or die with Hollis?"

"Ain't seen him yet," Cas lied, for he had just returned from a meeting with Mitt Brennan at the Alliance site. In truth, Cas had no intention whatsoever of confronting Mitt with a choice. Mitt was an ass-kisser, and Cas wouldn't abide being led by an ass-kisser.

No, he'd run this three-man outfit himself. And if there was as much minted gold in Hollis Blackburn's house as Cas hoped, hell, might be he'd just take it all for himself and light a shuck for San Francisco. A man with a stake could set himself up sweet in a city where big money could be made with few questions asked.

But first he had to kill Fargo. Until that bearded meddler was cut from the mix, Cas knew none of them was safe, no plan secure. Hollis Blackburn was right about that much, at least.

All three men emerged from the cave, Boyd's fancy spurs chinging, into an afternoon grown overcast and gusty. Narrow footpaths, as ancient as the paintings inside the cave, crisscrossed the sloping side of Spearfish Canyon behind plenty of tree cover. Each man headed for his prearranged position overlooking the trail below.

Cas, moving stiff-legged from his old injury, headed for an old dugout, a squat edifice of mud and lumber with its hind end backed into the canyon slope. Best Cas could figure, maybe early fur traders built it to fight off Sioux. It afforded an excellent view of the canyon floor below.

He made himself a little wallow in the soft dirt, laying the long muzzle of the Big Fifty through one of the firing ports. He lowered the breech block and inserted a round into the chamber.

By this time Fargo and his jury-rigged wagon were moving into perfect range. Cas lined up his sights just under Fargo's ear, then took a deep breath and slowly expelled it.

"You've seen your last sunrise, Fargo," he muttered as his finger took up the trigger slack.

Years of frontier survival had taught Fargo to rely on his ears as much as he did his eyes. With experience he had learned how to ignore the noises that naturally belonged to a place, concentrating instead on any sounds that didn't.

And right now he heard one that didn't.

It came to him sporadically, wafted on the wind gusts: a rhythmic, metallic sound, so faint he couldn't be sure it wasn't really some distant memory.

But it was a noise, one that didn't belong in the wild. Which meant it almost surely spelled trouble.

He suddenly turned around and leaned back on the seat to shout back at Doc and Colleen. Later, Fargo would realize it was that simple movement that saved his life.

The very moment he turned around, the crack of a rifle shot split the silence and echoed along the canyon walls. Something hot tickled the nape of Fargo's neck, and the board seat beside him splintered as a big-caliber slug chewed into it.

Fargo immediately leaped to the offside of the wagon, grabbing his Henry out of the bed as he sheltered behind the vehicle. Even before he had taken cover, shots erupted from the slope Fargo now faced. Rounds thwacked into the wagon, spooking the claybank. But the bullet-savvy Ovaro held fast.

Doc Boone's ginger hunkered on its hocks, terrified at the sudden racket. Fargo glanced quickly around. The nearest good shelter was about an eighth of a mile west of the trail, some sandbar willows near the creek. This meant more time lost, but there was no avoiding the delay.

"Doc!" he shouted. "Make for them willows near the creek!"

"Tell that to my goddamn horse, you chucklehead!" Boone roared back. "It's frozen in place!"

Fargo, ducking and dodging lead, picked up a rock and bounced it off the ginger's right shoulder. As he'd hoped, the horse bolted to the left.

"Fargo, you son of a bitch!" Boone's voice faded with the retreating buggy. "You not only get me killed, you force me to die sober! You Satanic bastard! . . ."

Fargo had been busy spotting muzzle flashes. There were three shooters about fifty yards apart. One, he realized after closer scrutiny, was firing from a crude dugout. A little out of range for the Henry.

Not so the one in the black slouch hat, who kept brazenly rising from behind a downed tree to plink at Fargo.

The Trailsman chambered a round, waited for a light lull in the firing, then quickly stood up for a second before covering down again.

The shooter took his bait, rising to snap off a round. Fargo dropped a quick bead, then raised the muzzle a hair—his sights were set for game, about two hundred yards. But the man behind the tree was at least three hundred fifty yards off.

Fargo plugged him high in the chest, and the man rolled, tumbled, bounced, and then just plain fell the final steep drop to the canyon floor. For the first few seconds, before life and sense were battered out of him, he screamed, a terrifying sound that silenced the other two guns.

Despite the overcast sky, Fargo saw the falling man's fancy silver spurs glint a few times. And suddenly he could name that repeated sound which warned him earlier: a spur wheel being snapped.

But Fargo knew he had to act immediately. The two partners of the man he'd just killed were momentarily shocked and unnerved, yes. In an eyeblink, however, those feelings could turn to bloodlust.

So he struck back quick. The Henry had almost a full tube, so he levered and fired, splitting his shots between the two remaining positions. One man (Fargo spotted a campaign hat with a yellow cavalry cord) was sheltered only in bushes, and he retreated after Fargo's first few shots.

The shooter in the dugout might have toughed it out longer if Fargo had not spotted the rifle ports and concentrated his shots there. Soon enough he saw a big man with a flat-crowned hat and a limping gait flee into the trees above the dugout. He must have met his friend at a rendezvous point, for a minute or so later Fargo heard two horses running along a hidden trail above them.

Another time and he would have tracked the men down. But right now he was racing against the ravages of mountain fever. His enemy was Time, and Fargo knew a bullet couldn't win that fight.

He waited a few more minutes, watching and listening. Then he climbed into the wagon and clucked to his reluctant team. They began hauling the broken-down wagon toward the creek and the stand of willows.

Five more miles of this, Fargo fretted. This was only the beginning, and who knew how many more rifles would eventually join the effort?

But a nervy little grin eased his lips apart. "What the hell, Fargo?" he muttered. "Did you expect to live forever?"

12

"Well, now you've got us here," Doc Boone challenged Fargo as the latter drove his rig into the shelter of the willows. "What's the plan?"

"That's one nut I haven't cracked yet," Fargo admitted as he wrapped the reins around the brake handle and swung down off the seat.

"Well *both* of mine have been cracked," Doc complained. "And I been shot at and captured by smelly savages and forced to ride bareback *and* had my liquor confiscated like contraband! On top alla that, I gotta watch you sniff around my niece like a stag in rut."

"Uncle Josh!" Colleen snapped. "You watch your coarse and vulgar mouth! Skye acts like more of a gentleman around me than you do."

"Hah! Now it's 'Skye,' is it?" The buggy tilted as Doc Boone climbed awkwardly out, grunting at the effort. "Sure sign he's had his way with you! Skipped the wedding and went right to the honeymoon. No wonder you're taking his part."

"Would you pipe down?" Fargo told him. "Your mouth runs like a spring river. A hundred mounted lancers could attack, and we'd never hear 'em over your constant belly-achin'."

"Lancers *will* attack, by God, you'll see to that! And Roman legions and Attila the Hun and Genghis Khan. Not to mention floods, tornadoes, and other acts of God or the devil. If there's danger, Fargo, you'll search it out and share it with those around you. What's that? Why not do things the easy and safe way? Not on your tintype, mister! Glory-seeking Skye Fargo will gladly get you killed."

Fargo waved the ranting old man off and dug into a saddlebag until he located his brass-framed binoculars. It was frustrating to be this close, yet have to delay. But this was the final push, at the most dangerous point, and Fargo knew that even a quick scout could mean the margin of survival.

Just north of the willows was a stand of tall pine trees. Fargo picked one and shinnied up to the first solid branch, then started climbing. When he had a good vantage point, with the entire canyon spread out below like a painting on canvas, he began a methodical study with the binoculars.

Eventually he caught sight of two horsebackers and recognized, from their hats, the two ambushers who had gotten away. Not surprisingly they were headed south toward the Alliance Mine.

He raised the binoculars, adjusted focus, and suddenly had a good view of the mining site. The damage his blast had caused was immediately evident. Not only was the explosives shack missing, a hole in its place, but piles of rubble surrounding it were all that remained of several storage and equipment sheds.

Once again he took a moment to notice well the location of the stately brick house overlooking the mine—no doubt the residence of Hollis Blackburn, Mine Supervisor. When the right moment came, Fargo figured it was time to pay Hollis a little visit. And he definitely had no plans to send in his card first.

He was about to train the binoculars elsewhere when something else caught his eye—a formation of a few dozen men gathered in a clearing between two low bunkhouses. They were miners, clearly, pale-skinned men in ore-stained clothing. But a lantern-jawed man with old pox scars marring his face was issuing them repeating rifles, not picks and shovels.

Could be drill for defense against the Sioux, Fargo reasoned. Or just maybe Hollis Blackburn had other plans for those guns. . . .

Thinking of Blackburn made him swing the binoculars much closer to study the man he had shot. He'd need another one of Blackburn's toadies, captured alive, to get the proof he required to link Hollis to those dying Wyoming prospectors and the infected clothing. Proof in his own mind, if not in court.

He had already started climbing down, still sweeping the area through the binoculars, when something else caught his attention. A stagnant deadwater had formed behind the creek, and floating in it was a large raft made from notched logs lashed together. Fargo guessed it might have been abandoned some time ago in the creek and someone dragged it into the deadwater to clear it out of the way.

It was mostly hidden now by tangled brush. But he could make out a crude tiller, made from nailed shingles, and a willow-pole mast ready for a sail. The germ of an idea came to Fargo, and he immediately dismissed it as a hair-brained scheme. However, when he failed to come up with any alternatives, he decided even hair-brained action was better than none at all.

"I've got that plan you were asking about, Doc," he announced when he returned to the other two. "And it's a dilly. We're going to *float* the last five miles to Busted Hump."

"On what? Or do we just wade through your bullshit?"

"There's an abandoned raft on the other side of the

creek," Fargo replied. "Big one—there's even room for your mouth, Doc. We'll have to look it over. But I think it'll hold us, the horses, and the supplies. We'll have to abandon the vehicles, though. We'll hide your buggy here and get it when we can. That wagon ain't no loss—it's not even good kindling."

"Fargo, have you gone soft between your head handles? Look how slow that current is. Why not ride a glacier?"

Fargo pointed at the supply wagon with its missing wheel. "Slower than that? I'd wager that current runs four miles per hour, same speed a man walks. Besides, the raft's got a mast. We'll rig up a sail, make even better time."

"Hell, let's give it a paddle wheel, too," Doc jabbed. "And maybe we can rig up a steam whistle?"

"I trust your judgment, Skye," Colleen put in, frowning at her uncle. "But won't we be awfully . . . vulnerable out on the water like that?"

"No doubt of that," he admitted. "But near as I can figure it, that route's our best bet. The Alliance thugs will concentrate on the trail and the trees nearby, not the creek itself. Sure, we'll probably eventually be spotted by one of their lookouts. But it's only five miles—with a little luck, we'll reach Busted Hump before they can respond."

" 'With a little luck' my sweet aunt! It's a cock-eyed plan," Doc Boone pronounced.

"Maybe so. Let's hear yours."

Boone glowered, silent.

"I thought so," Fargo said. "Look, I admit my plan is dicey. But I'm also convinced we won't survive the trail. It's either the creek or give up. And while I stand here jawboning with you, more time's wasted. You two follow me. We've got to work fast."

Mitt Brennan had never seen his employer this nervous and agitated. Usually a man of cool, ironic command, Hollis Blackburn now paced back and forth in his study, eyes nervously flicking toward the windows. He was a scared man trying hard to cover up his fear.

"So Boyd is dead," he repeated Mitt's latest news. "And Cas and Orrin just turned tail and *ran*? The bloody, cowardly idiots! They picked a fine time to go wobbly. That means Fargo will almost surely get through to Busted Hump with that infernal doctor."

Hollis, fingers nervously twirling the tips of his waxed mustache, quickened his pacing.

"Is the raid all set?" he demanded.

Mitt patiently nodded. He sat in a fancy wing chair, his hat balanced on his knee. Secretly, the Englishman's obvious fear disturbed Mitt. They had just covered all these details, but Hollis was so distracted he didn't even remember they'd done it.

"The men have been picked and rifles and ammo belts issued," Mitt reported again.

"They know exactly what they're to do?"

"They understand completely. No survivors."

Hollis caught something in the other man's tone—some nuance he didn't like.

"There were problems with that?" he demanded.

Mitt's gaze shifted to his own toes. "Some of the men drew the line at women and kids. They were let go. But at the rate you're paying, we had enough volunteers to take their place."

"All right," Hollis said. "I want you to attack at first light tomorrow. Don't forget to pry off the horse shoes before you ride out. And shoot some arrows into the dead bodies. Take a few scalps, too. We need enough evidence to hang it on the Sioux."

Mitt fidgeted and looked uncomfortable.

"What is it now?" Hollis demanded.

"Well, I know it's not my place to say, Mr. Blackburn. But some of the men are . . . squeamish, you might say, about the scalping and mutilation stuff. The killing is fine, but that other . . . is it really necessary?"

"Definitely," Hollis assured him. "We need to create 'lies like truth.' That's what is required to prevail under law. Don't worry about the raid tomorrow. Worry about Fargo. Because I'll tell you right now—so long as he's alive, you and I and Suzette stand no chance of meeting that flatboat at Bridger's Landing on the Belle Fourche. That man is implacable as destiny. He's proved it in the past few days."

Hollis paused in the embrasure of a window, gazing out at the increasingly cloudy sky. Dark thunderheads were piling up around the highest peaks of the forested Black Hills. It was a sight he'd noticed before plenty of times. Now, though, it seemed like a portent of disaster.

"It's peculiar, Mitt," he mused. "I've never been what you'd call a superstitious person. But the moment I learned Fargo had found those dying prospectors, I had a bad feeling that our cake was dough. *How* can one man thwart the ambitions of so many? It's as if his arrival has even stirred the Sioux into swifter action. I know this much: gold mining, in the Black Hills, is about to go violently out of fashion for some time to come."

"Don't worry," Mitt assured him. "We can't do much about the Sioux. But we'll bait Fargo out."

"Yes," Hollis agreed softly, still gazing out the window. "But just *who* will be the bait?"

"*Wheee*! There it goes!" Colleen shouted in delight as the first good wind filled their makeshift sail. "I can already feel us picking up speed."

Fargo, operating the tiller at the rear of the raft, had to grin at the spectacle they presented: three tired and rumpled humans, three confused horses, and a heap of supplies, all sailing on a ridiculous-looking, half-waterlogged old raft in a creek barely wide enough, in places, to float it.

The wooden rudder connected to the tiller that moved it was half-rotted away. This cut down on steering ability and forced Fargo to now and then lean on a long willow pole to free them from a mudbank. The sail was a huge bolt of sturdy wagon canvas taken from the supplies. Fargo had brought it in hopes of encouraging the residents of Busted Hump to evacuate as soon as possible.

"Stupidest damn idea I ever heard of," Doc Boone grumped. "And I've heard some lulus."

He was hunched down inside a little sheltered area Fargo had made from the supplies. "This damn raft could have belonged to Lewis and Clark, it's that old. Look there how these lashings are almost rotted away. We'll break up and sink within the next half mile."

"Sink?" Colleen repeated, tossing back her head to laugh. "Why, Uncle Josh! This creek is barely over my shoulders at its deepest."

"I ain't planning to cross the Pacific," Fargo reminded

him. "This old hunk of driftwood only needs to float us a little over an hour or so."

"Won't matter," Doc insisted. "If we don't sink, we'll all be shot."

"Don't worry, Doc," Fargo said, aiming a wink at Colleen. "Anything happens to you, I'll take good care of your niece."

That set the irascible old medico off on another hot string of curses and complaints. Fargo ignored him, keeping his eyes to both sides of Spearfish Creek. In places the creek widened considerably, making room for small islands covered with cottonwoods. He studied these with special care, his Henry leaning against a nearby crate.

". . . another thing," Doc Boone was still raging, wagging a pudgy finger at him. "My buggy *better* be there when we return for it, mister. It was custom-made for me in Omaha."

"If it ain't, you'll be paid for it, you old windbag," Fargo said. "Give that mouth of yours a rest."

"Go *rest* in hell, Fargo! You dang well better pay me! I still got my shotgun to home. Can't even get a goddamn drink . . . you worthless, skirt-chasing. . . ."

Still grumbling, Doc curled up and was soon snoring like a man without a trouble in the world.

"You oughta crawl in there with him," Fargo suggested to Colleen. "It'll be safer if there's any shooting."

She flashed a smiling mouthful of perfect teeth that gleamed like pearls. She ain't wasting her time with that hog-bristle toothbrush, Fargo admitted to himself. Nicest teeth he'd ever seen.

"Are you kidding?" she replied. "I'll take my chances with bullets. I'd rather crawl into a bear's den than crowd Uncle Josh. You think we're going to make it, Skye?"

"I always think that," he replied cheerfully.

"Seriously. You know what I mean. Not philosophy or outlook. I mean right now, this terrible situation—you really think we're going to be all right?"

He nodded. "I do. I can hear them calling to each other out by the trail. They can't figure out where we are, but it's fixed in their minds that we have two vehicles. I don't think they'll check the creek in time, and even if they do, they might not check our part of it. They didn't expect us to find a raft. Problem is, to be honest with you, our troubles ain't over even when we get there."

"I know. I listened to what those Sioux braves told us. But I trust you to do the right thing," she assured him. She added, flushing a little after she said it: "You certainly did all the right things earlier, when we were alone together. I can't stop thinking about it."

Fargo grinned. "I aim to please, ma'am."

"Only one complaint," she added. "I want more."

"What man has done," he assured her, "man will do. With pleasure."

"You liked it, too?" she pressed.

"Did you get some other impression?" he teased her. "Look, if you keep reminding me of it, I'm gonna have trouble standing up straight. That answer your question?"

"*Good.* I like to make that happen to you. It gets me all excited."

"Speaking of that," Fargo warned, "you best hush. I'm on the feather edge."

She laughed, delighting in her own naughtiness and feminine power. Fargo watched her trail her bare feet over the edge of the raft. Her dress was pulled up almost to midthigh—slender, shapely thighs, creamy white and supple. Her cinnamon hair was no longer in plaits but tumbled loose over her shoulders, thick and curly.

Reluctantly he raised his gaze to watch the onsweep of dark clouds—it looked like there was some rough weather brewing up west of the Black Hills.

"Storm makin' up," he told Colleen. "There's an oilcloth rain slicker in my blanket roll. You better have it ready. Looks like we're gonna get a gully-washer."

She did as he suggested, crossing the raft toward him. But after she dug the slicker out, instead of returning to her spot she pressed close to Fargo, filling his nostrils with the odor of her lilac perfume.

"You felt *so* good inside me," she cooed, her low velvet voice caressing his ear. "So big and hard, just all man and filling up my girl place. I get all trembly just thinking about it."

He had his hand on the tiller, so that's where she suddenly put hers—on *his* tiller. She rubbed him, egging him on with urgent, ardent talk.

"Oh, lord, Skye, it's growing huge right in my hand. Oh, I can't . . . I shouldn't . . . not *here*! . . ."

She was arguing with herself, not him, and the horny part of her won. At first Fargo really intended to stop her when she crouched before him and fumbled open his trousers. This was not the place and time to play. But once he felt the hot, wet pleasure of her mouth taking him in, his will power was shot all to hell.

"Damn, girl, that ain't fair," he moaned. "But it sure is nice. Do what you gotta."

Her head moved faster, faster, and Fargo felt his legs going wobbly as the pleasure waves built.

"Mmm," she moaned, using her hand now, too, for the part she couldn't fit into her mouth.

His vision glazed, the day went blurry, pleasure weakened him all over. Fargo staggered backward as he spent himself, unaware until too late that he had caught his balance by grabbing the tiller and turning the raft hard toward shore.

There was a sudden, hard thud and a jarring lurch that brought some supply boxes crashing down around the sleeping Doc Boone. He woke up screeching. "Don't scalp me, I'm bald!"

Then he saw his niece kneeling near Fargo, Fargo with his back turned, fumbling with his trousers. One corner of the raft had run aground on a gravel bank. Boone's beard-scruffed face flushed purple, and Fargo saw him working up to his first string of curses.

Just then, however, nature intervened dramatically.

The rain-swollen belly of the sky abruptly burst, releasing a sudden, heavy gray curtain of water that seemed to be hurling itself at them, not just raining. It was followed by a cracking, stuttering rumble of thunder and an explosive burst of skeletal lightning. Fargo played hell settling the horses before their hoofs broke up the raft.

Cursing himself for a lustful fool, he sent Colleen to huddle with her uncle under the rain slicker. Fargo leaned into the willow pole, heaving them back out into the rain-pimpled creek. The sail was useless now, but this heavy downpour would quicken the current.

He felt ashamed for giving in to his urges now, with time running out. The afternoon was well advanced, and there was very little time left on his critical seventy-two-hour deadline.

His hair and clothes already rain-plastered to him, Fargo steered them back out into the current, hoping he wasn't too late—hoping Busted Hump would still be there, not just a pile of ashes and charred bones.

13

"Land sakes alive! What in tarnal blazes is *that*?"

The sudden, heavy, but quick downpour had ended, and Mary Ellen Guidry had gone down to the bathing pool to wash her beautiful blonde hair. She loved to fluff it all out while men stared.

Now, however, she gazed open-mouthed through a wall of reeds as the shaky old raft slid past her, a drenched Skye Fargo at the tiller. Then one of the horses shifted, and Mary Ellen saw the pretty, cinnamon-haired girl with Skye.

"Me and him brought down a whole shack makin' whoopee," she steamed out loud. "Now he comes back flauntin' *another* hussy right 'fore my very eyes? I'll kick that man so hard in the jewels he'll *never* have a family!"

She hurried toward the opposite bank, where more and more residents of Busted Hump were excitedly congregating.

Fargo nudged the raft into shore, where Powhatan Stone and several other men quickly tied it off. Elijah, his face a mask of deep worry lines, was the first to grip Fargo's hand.

"You cut it close," the big prospector greeted him. "But it's a miracle you even got through."

Elijah turned immediately to grab Doc Boone's medical bag and help him off the raft. "Jesus, Doc, are you ever a welcome sight. *Please* hurry! They're all over here in the pesthouse. We ain't lost nobody yet, but some of 'em are off their heads. Ranting and raving."

"Tell him why we're late, Fargo," Doc Boone snapped,

sending an icy stare toward the Trailsman. "Tell him how we all got sidetracked while you went tripping down the Primrose Path."

But Elijah practically dragged Doc Boone off. As Fargo offered his arm to Colleen, helping her ashore, he spotted a dour-faced Mary Ellen Guidry shooting daggers at him from angry blue eyes. *There's trouble*, he told himself. Right now, however, there were bigger fish to fry.

Colleen, who like Doc Boone had already taken the protective dose of diluted carbolic, hurried toward the pesthouse to help her uncle begin the treatment. Fargo was leading the horses ashore when he spotted con man Philly Tyler at the edge of the crowd. As usual he was the only one decked out in going-to-town duds, although the needless chaps made him look ridiculous.

"Good work, Fargo," Philly called out to him. "And that was some fireworks show night before last."

Fargo, leading the horses, crossed to where the grifter stood. "You know, Philly, I commence to wonder why a fellow with your talent for skinning wallets is working a place this dangerous? You don't strike me as the rough frontier type. Dandified chaps like you require clean sheets and gaslights."

Philly's round, smooth-shaven face revealed nothing. "Why, Fargo, I'm cut deep. Are you implying that I am a deceitful and cynical man?"

He reached into the voluminous folds of his frock coat and produced a little chunk of varnished wood.

"Today, f'rinstance, I'm offering a special on pieces of wood cut from the very cross on which our Lord was crucified. Each piece numbered and issued with a certificate of authenticity signed by the Pope himself. Only ten dollars, Fargo, for a literal piece of history."

A weary Fargo shook his head, unable to resist a grin. "I swear, Philly, you'd cheat a war widow. You are the world-beatingest man to figure out. I won't lie to you. It's crossed my mind that you and Hollis Blackburn could be feeding from the same trough."

That finally coaxed a grin out of the poker-faced con artist. "Right. Just like these hunks of wood really came from the Cross instead of an old outhouse in Iowa."

"I may regret this," Fargo told him before moving on. "But I've got too much on my plate as it is, so I've decided to trust you. You're up to something, all right, and somehow it involves Blackburn. But looks like we'll just have to play this game through."

"Skye!" Pow called out behind him, where he was busy organizing the unloading of supplies. "You, the doc, and that pretty nurse can have my shack. I'm bunking with Elijah. Grab you some shut-eye—man, you've earned it."

Fargo had to agree. He'd just spent three of the most harrowing days of his life. And he'd barely slept in the past four days. He ought to feel proud of what he'd accomplished, but he couldn't shake the memory of that formation he'd spotted earlier at the Alliance site. And these folks at Busted Hump *had* to be woken up to the imminent threat from the Sioux. Any way he sliced it, Fargo saw this place as a deathtrap—one from which the locals needed to escape as soon as possible.

But those arguments, and everything else, would have to wait. He had resisted weariness when he had to, but right now Fargo was practically staggering. He was grateful when one of the prospectors took over the horses for him. He barely made it up the slope to Pow's shanty before collapsing on the shuck mattress, too exhausted to even remove his gun and boots.

"A guard detail ain't enough," Fargo insisted to the others, trying to stay patient with these men who had done little soldiering. "Sentries are fine for routine security *if* you got a strong fighting force to back them. But some of your best men are being treated right now for fever, and Elijah tells me fifty of your number are women and children. 'Sides all that, very few of you have repeating weapons."

Fargo waited for those words to sink in.

"If what I'm afraid is coming does come," he resumed, "it will likely be at first light tomorrow. A strong, well-armed force paid top dollar to kill and issued repeating rifles to do it effectively. Against a force like that, guards alone will accomplish only one thing: warn us all that it's time to die."

His words were grim. But they came from the same man who had just fed the camp and given it new hope. So they listened carefully, giving each of his words great weight. There were ten of them, selected by the camp's unofficial constables, Elijah and Powhatan Stone. Fargo had slept deeply for the past six hours, wolfed down a meal, then asked the Stone brothers to call this meeting outside the corral.

"If guards ain't enough," said a voice in the shadowy darkness, "what else do we need?"

"Siege defenses," Fargo told him. "This position is excellent for them. They can be done cheap, they can be done quick, they confound and weaken our enemy without costing us a bullet."

"Sure, Mr. Fargo, but we ain't army men," said another prospector. "You're talking stuff like them West Point engineers learn. We know ore and veins and such. No disrespect, but how can we even be sure Hollis Blackburn has ordered an attack for dawn?"

"We can't," Fargo admitted. "But think like your enemy. Hollis knows the doctor is here, which means the camp gets stronger the longer Hollis waits. Maybe I'm wrong on the day. But those rifles weren't being issued for a parade."

"Hell yes," Elijah put in. Like several other men present he was leaning on the top pole of the corral. "And you got to bear in mind, Hank, all the rest that's been done to us. The flooding, the poisoned water, the infected duds, hell, even setting a rabid wolf loose on our dogs! To Hollis Blackburn, people like us ain't nothing but cockroaches. He figures he's quality folk, he can stomp on us. I ain't seen Skye be wrong yet. I say the fight's coming to us at dawn."

"We've got all night to prepare," Fargo reminded them. "Plenty of time if we stay frosty and work hard. We don't need no fancy West Point boys, just strong backs. And even though you'll be working, try to keep those backs to a wall and your weapons to hand. Some of these bullyboys like to hit in the dead of night, burn down a sleeping camp. Moon's in third quarter, that gives them plenty of light later on when the clouds blow over."

The specific work crews were appointed, one for each set of siege defenses. Fargo assigned one crew to take their pick-axes and gouge out "trip holes" throughout the steep, grassy slope descending toward Busted Hump. Holes hard to spot and just big enough for a charging horse's ankle to plunge into.

Another crew was assigned to cut and sharpen long, narrow stakes. Sharpened at both ends, then driven deep underground in high grass at a slant, they could be effective at impaling a charging horse in dim light. Fargo loathed treating a horse that way, but after all they would be carrying an enemy bent on brutal murder. This was about survival.

He also ordered a wide trench to be dug around the inner circle of the camp, where the women, children, and sick would be hunkered down. It didn't need to be dug deep. Just a trench too wide to jump and too softened up and rock-strewn to charge through without difficulty.

He agreed to move around throughout the night, supervising the work. Fargo welcomed that job anyway because it gave him a chance to keep a trained scout's eye on things in the area. These men were stout and brave enough, all right, and formidable saloon brawlers. But they were babes in the woods when it came to organized battle tactics or effective scouting.

Before the meeting broke up, Philly Tyler walked up to join the group, smoking a fat cigar.

"What's the latest from the pesthouse?" Fargo asked.

"I'm told that doctor you brought is some pumpkins," Philly replied. "And his nurse is as efficient as she is beautiful. It's too early still to say how it's going. But neither one of those two has stopped working since they got here."

Fargo wasn't surprised to learn that about Colleen—the milk of human kindness flowed through her veins. But *vinegar* flowed through Doc Boone's. And yet, when sober anyway, it appeared he was a dedicated and skilled doctor.

"Maybe I was a mite rough on the old scutter," he mused. "They been fed, at least?"

"That, and they're gettin' plenty of coffee," Pow assured him. "Thanks to your supply run, Skye."

"All right, sourdoughs!" Elijah called out. " 'Nuff said! We got our marching orders. Let's get a nice little reception set up for our visitors from the Alliance."

Fargo left his Ovaro in the corral for a well-deserved rest. He patrolled the entire area on foot, his Henry and Colt freshly cleaned and oiled.

The work crews performed as Fargo knew they would— efficiently and well. These men were used to backbreaking labor, and within a few hours only the final siege trench remained unfinished. The other workers joined that crew without being ordered to.

Fargo doubted that the enemy would attack from any other direction. The terrain would force them to split up. These attackers would want the safety and "crazy brave" bravado of the pack, the blood-tingling thunder of many charging hoofs. That meant attacking en masse down the slope from above.

While he circled the area, Fargo kept an eye peeled for that rabid wolf. By now it might have crawled off to die, but he took no chances. However, he also kept his eye out for any game. Despite his supply delivery, what the camp still lacked was fresh meat.

So he made a point of wandering down to the moonlit creek now and then. That's where he spotted the pronghorn buck, drinking along the far bank about a hundred yards south of camp. The meat's tough, he reminded himself. Still, it was better and more nourishing than rabbit stew.

He knew better than to move any closer. Moving slowly and avoiding any sudden motions, Fargo stooped into a kneeling offhand position. He dropped the buck clean with one shot.

"It's Fargo!" he shouted to calm jittery nerves after the sound of the shot. "Just putting meat on the table!"

He bled and rough-gutted his kill right on the spot, leaving the innards for the grateful camp dogs. Then he slung the buck's carcass over his shoulders and hauled it out front of Pow's cabin. Working in the generous moonlight, he dressed it out proper in cuts ready to cook. These he wrapped in cheesecloth and carried back to the springhouse near the creek to keep the meat cool.

All this activity was interspersed with more quick foot patrols. But Fargo spotted no sign yet of Alliance riders or spies. He figured he'd find out soon enough if his hunch was right—the sky to the east now glowed with false dawn, meaning the real thing wasn't far off.

It was time now to talk with Elijah and Pow about placement of the defenders. Fargo didn't want them clustered. Instinct made men bunch up when frightened, but often that only made them easier for their enemy to kill.

He found Pow quickly, but Elijah was nowhere they

looked. They finally located him off by himself beside the chuckling creek, evidently in a daze.

" 'Lijah!" Pow called to him, his tone worried. "You up to fettle, big brother?"

Elijah looked at both men, unashamed of the tears streaking his cheeks.

"Aww, hell, Elijah," Pow stammered, about to cry himself. "It's Jimmy, ain't it? Brother, I'm sorry."

"For what, little brother?" Elijah exclaimed jubilantly. "My boy just woke up, clear-headed and hungry as a winter-starved bear! Hallelujah, boys!"

Pow whooped loudly, somehow picking up his huge sibling and twirling him around. Fargo smiled, happy for Elijah and Jimmy, immensely proud of Doc Boone and Colleen.

"They finally get some rest?" Fargo asked. "Doc and his niece, I mean."

Elijah nodded. "Yes, God bless 'em. Said they done what they can for now. They think Dotty caught it late enough she's gonna be fine. Some of the first to get sick—now, they might be more iffy. Doc says one or two might not make it, but most will."

"It's good news," Fargo agreed. "Now maybe we got another fight coming. Roust out the sleepers and have 'em look to their weapons. Each man should fan out and set up in some kind of sheltered position. I like a big tree, myself, because you can move around it as your targets shift. *No*body shoots until his bead is plumb. Every man should also have a blade of some kind—there *will* be ground fighting when riders get tossed, there always is."

"You've done this plenty, ain't you?" Pow said admiringly.

"More than I'd prefer to," Fargo admitted. He turned to gaze in the direction of the Alliance Mine. "I guess you might say I just ain't cut out for school teaching."

Hollis Blackburn stood in the big bay window of his upstairs bedroom, gazing out at the gathering light.

"Hollees," Suzette called to him from their big canopied bed, "*pleez* come to bed? You have stand there all night."

"No point in going to bed now," he told her. "The attack

begins soon. Once Mitt gets back here, we'll have to start packing to meet that flatboat. Unless. . . ."

"Unless? Unless what?"

Hollis turned and began pacing back and forth in the darkened room. "Unless that goddamn Skye Fargo survives. If he does, we'll never bloody make it out of here."

"But, Hollees, why do you say such a thing? He is only one man. You have defeat so many."

That much was certainly true, Hollis told himself. He had decided, early on in life, that a man cannot conquer the world from his own front yard. So he had gone abroad to practice his brand of mastery over men. And along the way he made many widows and orphans. But men like Skye Fargo were new to his experience.

"You don't understand, Suzette . . . Fargo symbolizes what the Yanks like to call 'a reckoning.' *My* reckoning. And I've never even met the man, that's what makes it so amazing. He just came out of nowhere like some avenging angel. He's not just a man—he's retribution. He's destiny. *My* destiny."

Suddenly, below his window, Hollis heard the thundering of many hoofs. He hurried to the window and glanced out. Mitt Brennan's strike force flashed by below, headed toward Busted Hump. The sight filled him with a bold new confidence.

"The fat's in the fire now," he muttered to himself. "I'll sink you yet, Fargo. Sink you six feet closer to hell!"

14

They attacked out of the rising sun, about fifty men strong, well horsed and well armed, confident of swift, certain, and ruthless victory over a sleeping foe.

At the first sound of their approach Fargo had been confused, for he immediately recognized the distinctive thump of unshod horses. Then, when he first spotted the attackers,

he understood. Some had bows and arrows with them—
Hollis Blackburn planned to pin this expected slaughter on
the Sioux.

Some of the attackers shouted war cries to rally their comrades. Armed with repeating rifles and plenty of ammo in
crossed bandoleers, these men did not have to hoard their
shots. They opened up even before they were within effective
range. So many rifles firing at once, and so rapidly, made a
sound like a giant ice floe breaking apart. An almost literal
wall of lead poured down on the camp, thwacking into dwellings, stripping bushes, kicking up geysers of dirt. Fargo heard
a woman scream and hoped it was only fright.

"Hold your fire until my command!" he bellowed above
the noise of the charge.

Pow and Elijah repeated the order to the men in their
battle groups. The defenders had set up three reinforced
positions behind the final siege defense, the softened
trench. Fargo, hunkered down behind a low pile of rocks,
planned to let the other siege defenses thin out and dis-
hearten the enemy before firing the first shot in defense.
Target discipline would be crucial because most of the prospectors were armed with older, one-shot percussion weapons. One even toted a Colonial-era flintlock.

But right now the first line of defense, those hidden trip
holes, was doing its job well.

"*Whoop*-dee-diddly-*doo*!" Pow sang out as a big,
seventeen-hand quarter horse suddenly plunged earthward
at a full gallop, throwing its rider hard and then crushing
him as it rolled.

This sudden obstacle triggered a confused pileup as several more horses and their riders charged headlong into
the fallen.

By now Fargo had spotted the leader on his handsome
sorrel: the same long-jawed, pox-scarred man he had seen
through his binoculars yesterday, passing rifles out to
these marauders.

And evidently he had some battle savvy. Fargo watched
as the man skillfully divided his attack force, sending them
wide to both flanks to avoid the trip holes. However, that
was exactly where Fargo had ordered most of the pointed
stakes planted, anticipating this move.

There was a sudden, horrifying scream as a powerful

chestnut gelding caught one of the stakes in its intestines, driving it deep. The abrupt stop sent the rider flying headlong, snapping his neck upon impact.

It sickened Fargo to watch it, knowing he himself ordered stakes planted. But what sickened him even more was the thought of this entire camp, and especially all the human beings in it, being exterminated. Burned out like Russian thistles by murdering cowards willing to kill children in their beds. Fargo hated to hurt a horse, but he gave the order and he had no regrets. He had lives to save against damn long odds.

"Too bad about the horse," said a voice at Fargo's elbow. "But it died quick. All's fair in love and war, eh?"

Fargo glanced at Philly Tyler. Here was yet another surprise about the man. Bullets made the air fairly hum around their ears. But instead of hunkering down, as most of the defenders were wisely doing, Philly stood right out exposed. Yet, he had no weapon to hand and evidently meant to take no part in the battle.

Instead, he seemed intent on studying faces, as if searching for one man among the attackers.

"If you're looking for Hollis Blackburn," Fargo said above the din, "you didn't really expect him to face danger, did you?"

Philly glanced at him. "No," he admitted. "But I was hoping he'd come along to watch the destruction. He likes to do that sometimes. The man has an almost scientific interest in death."

A round flumped into Philly's dude hat, knocking it off his head, feather and all. The man didn't even flinch.

"So you know him, do you?" Fargo said.

Philly nodded. "Oh, I know him, all right."

"What's between you two?"

Philly picked up his hat, dusted it off, and plunked it back on his head.

"Personal matter," he replied, strolling away as if he were now bored with the battle and ready to have his morning coffee.

But Fargo had no time to wonder about the mystery. The first handful of attackers had gotten past the trip holes and the sharpened stakes. Now they raced across the last open stretch, rifle muzzles spitting fire and lead.

"Open fire!" Fargo roared, and a withering volley from the camp thinned out the first group of attackers.

But a big man with a nasty scar on his cheek seemed to recognize Fargo and aim straight for his position, firing as fast as he could lever his rifle. Fargo recognized him, by his flat-crowned hat, as one of the three ambushers from yesterday near the creek. He muttered a curse, for he wanted to capture one of the two survivors alive. But this one required killing, and quick.

Ignoring the slugs chunking in all around him, Fargo aimed for the man's lights, fired, and missed when he bucked the gun. But his next shot wiped him out of the saddle.

Fortunately, Fargo saw, there might be a chance to nab the other one. The attackers were already being routed. At least ten of their number lay dead or grievously wounded, and even as Fargo watched, the leader on the handsome sorrel caught a bullet in his side. Just as Fargo had hoped, the first siege defenses, and a spirited return fire from the prospectors, had combined to demoralize the Alliance riders.

But it was his "last-stand ditch" that finally snapped the back of the attack. As soon as the riders hit it, their horses floundered in the soft earth, stumbling, slowing down. This made their riders easy targets. Hardly more than five minutes after it began, the attack had clearly failed. The riders were slipping off in every direction, every man for himself.

"Done and *done*!" Elijah shouted, and a cheer erupted from the men.

Not quite done, Fargo told himself as he sprang up from cover and scrutinized the fleeing men. Then he spotted the familiar campaign hat with its yellow cavalry cord—the surviving member of that trio of ambushers.

Fargo didn't have much time, and it was a tricky shot. He only wanted to knock him out of the saddle, not kill him. He drew a bead high on the man's left shoulder, hit him, spun him, but the rider hung on, one hand gripping the saddle horn. Cursing, Fargo tossed a second shot in the same spot, and that dropped his man.

Fargo sprinted out to retrieve him, Colt drawn, then sent for Doc Boone to patch the man's wounds—otherwise the prisoner was in danger of bleeding out.

"What about their dead?" Pow asked him while Doc worked on their prisoner and Colleen tended to a couple of the defenders who'd been slightly wounded.

Fargo gazed out at the sloping battlefield. They had taken their wounded, probably for legal reasons more than humane ones. But the slope was strewn with their dead.

"They don't deserve Christian rites," Fargo said. "But I suggest tossing 'em in a giant grave to avoid the stink and vultures, and to spare your women and kids the sight. Cover it good with rocks or varmints'll dig 'em up."

For a moment Fargo just stood there in the middle of the camp, marveling, as he always did after a large battle, how unreal it always seemed right after it was over. Blue gun smoke still hazed the area, yes, and the acrid stink of spent powder stained the air. But a peaceful stillness had set in, and he could hear Spearfish Creek behind him, merrily bubbling as always. He glanced toward the corral and watched his Ovaro shake out the night kinks with a few moments of serious bucking. The racket was over, life went on. Moments earlier men had been locked in life-and-death combat; now it was all as unreal as an old man's fading memories.

Doc Boone emerged from the shack where the prisoner was being held under armed guard.

"He's all yours, Fargo," Doc said. "Now, if you're done inflicting death and destruction for the time being, I need to check on the fever patients."

Fargo nodded and headed toward the shack.

"What are you trying to find out from him?" Doc added from behind him. "He looks pretty stupid, to me."

"Just looking to tie up some loose ends," Fargo replied. "He's smart enough for my needs. And if he ain't, I'll smarten him up a little."

The man said his name was Orrin Jones and that he hailed from Arkansas, although until recently he'd been working as a trail guide, as he called it, out in the South Pass country. Fargo, sitting backwards on a kitchen chair, took in the Apache-style, knee-length moccasins. Jones lay facedown on a crude pallet, bare to the waist. The back of his left shoulder was so shot up the arm hung useless.

"You don't amount up to much, Jones," Fargo said.

"Ugly as proud flesh and a coward to boot. Yesterday you tried to kill me from ambush, this morning you intended to kill folks in their beds. You know, you boys were all holler and no heart. S'matter, you didn't expect any trouble slaughtering the women and kids? Especially you with that fancy 20-shot magazine rifle of yours."

Jones spoke in hissing bursts through teeth clenched in pain. "Sir, you got it all twisted around hindside foremost. I'm just one a the miners. Our foreman, he ordered a bunch of us—"

"That's a bald-faced lie," Fargo cut in. "I s'pose you wear them moccasins down in the mine? Nothing ruins truth like stretching it, Jones. I want the truth and I want it now."

"I'd never try to lie to a man of your caliber, sir."

"Then don't try to soft soap me, either, you woman-killing cockroach. And if you think you're being humorous, I'm not in a funning mood."

"*You* ain't? Christ, you could drive a steamboat through the hole in me! That goddamn doc wouldn't even give me a nip for the pain, cussed me out and said to ask you why he had no whiskey."

"Never mind that," Fargo said. "He's got laudanum. If I decide you're coming clean with me, I'll tell him to come dose you."

"Square deal?"

"Best deal you'll get in *this* camp, you lily-livered mange pot. Now talk out."

"Well . . . you had it right, I was one of the three what tried to air you out yestiddy. But honest to God, mister, I was agin' this raid from the start. Cas Merrill will bear me out on that—I seen you got his horse. Mayhap he's one of your prisoners. Ask him—killing women and kids ain't in my line."

"He the one with the scarred cheek?"

Jones nodded, his face twisted in pain.

"He ain't too talkative anymore," Fargo said. "If you take my meaning? Here's how I see it. You, the one with the gaudy spurs, scar cheek—you three were Hollis Black-burn's personal night riders. Only, you took your orders through the jasper who led the attack this morning. That the way of it?"

Jones hesitated.

"I don't chew my cabbage twice, mister. You want me to send for that doc again 'r not?" Fargo demanded. "You're still oozing blood like a stuck pig."

"Yeah, you got it right," Jones finally admitted. "Hollis is the big bushway. The orders are passed on through Mitt Brennan, the one you saw leading the attack. We're all on Hollis's . . . whatchacallit, personal payroll, sorter."

"And you're certain," Fargo pressed, "that it was Hollis who gave the order to infect this camp with mountain fever?"

Jones averted his eyes. " 'Course it was him. Only high-born people like him can give orders like that."

It amazed and disgusted Fargo how so many low reptiles like Jones were in such awe of supposed "high birth." Rank, in Fargo's view of things, should be based on achievement, not birth. And getting rich through cold-blooded murder didn't count as an achievement.

Fargo turned to leave.

"Hey, wait!" Jones called out. "What about that doc? I'm in a powerful lot of pain here."

"He'll get to you when he's done tending to the decent," Fargo replied as he stepped outside.

He paused for a moment to stare out at the dead men and horses. The Vulture God—that's what Kills in Water called Hollis Blackburn. Men of his ilk always hired out their dirty work. Maybe what they needed was to have *their* noses rubbed in the blood for a change. . . .

Fargo made up his mind. Come hell or high water, he meant to settle some accounts with Hollis Blackburn. But as he started to angle up toward the corral, Colleen called his name.

"Skye! I see you're limping again. Let me have a look at that wound to your leg. The bandage hasn't been changed since Uncle Josh put it on, and I doubt if you've been keeping it clean."

Fargo would have skipped it except that the wound *did* itch considerably. And he knew better than to risk infection in country this remote.

He fell into step beside her and they headed toward Pow's cabin.

"That sounded like some battle," she remarked. "It scared the daylights out of me. I was hiding under a table."

"How's it going in the pesthouse?" he asked her.

"Still more folks recovering, thank God. We made it just in time. One person did pass away, but I think that's going to be the only loss."

They entered the shack, and she pulled in the latchstring so the door couldn't be opened from outside.

"Okay, you handsome rogue—drop 'em."

She meant his trousers. A wide grin split his face.

"Yes'm," he replied, hurrying to comply.

"Don't get that mischievous gleam in your eye, Skye Fargo! My will-power around you is weak, and this is no time to tempt me. If Uncle Josh comes back here and catches us, lord! Just turn around and get that big, beautiful thing out of my sight before I give in."

Reluctantly, Fargo did as told.

"My stars!" she scolded him. "It's not infected, but lord knows why not—it's caked with old, filthy blood. I'll have to scrape that out until it's bleeding fresh. This will hurt a bit. . . ."

She was just finishing applying a new dressing when Fargo heard Elijah's voice outside.

"Skye! Riders coming in under a truce flag!"

Fargo went outside. Three riders approached under a white flag.

"We're a delegation from the Alliance," one of them called out. "We want you folks to know that most of us miners had nothing to do with what happened here today."

Fargo nodded. "I believe you, friend. But let me give you some advice for your own safety: You and the rest get out *now*. The Sioux are painted for war, and they mean to purge these hills of all whiteskins."

The miner pointed toward the eastern sky. Dark puffs of signal smoke rose above the rounded peaks of the Black Hills.

"We just figured that out. They been signaling each other all morning. Us miners are getting the hell out. You folks better, too."

As the delegation rode off, Fargo headed toward the corral.

"What's on the spit?" Elijah shouted to him.

"I got a little visit to pay," Fargo answered. "I'm prob'ly too late. But I want to make sure."

"Make sure of what?"

"That justice gets done," he replied. "And in the absence of any law, that's all we got: *just us.*"

Fargo took the canyon trail to the Alliance Mine, ready for trouble but suspecting the danger from Alliance thugs was over. Two of them were dead, another a prisoner. Even the one who escaped earlier, Mitt Brennan, was seriously wounded.

He reached the site without incident and saw, from the encircling pines, that the scene was bedlam. Miners scurried everywhere, packing up their possessions and preparing to leave. Every available dray animal and ore wagon had been rounded up and pressed into service. And none too soon: dark smoke signals still floated across the eastern sky, spelling imminent doom for any fool who stayed in these hills.

Keeping out of sight in the trees, Fargo circled around to the lone house on its little grassy rise behind the mine. He left the Ovaro tethered in the trees and crossed the yard to the rear of the house.

He entered through the kitchen. From habit when entering a dwelling, he scraped the mud off his boots on a chair edge. He knew by now that he wouldn't find Hollis Blackburn. His hunch was confirmed when he pushed open the door to the main house: the entire place had been ransacked. And the red-stained clay tracked everywhere told him it was miners who had been here.

Lamps lay broken; drawers had been pulled out from desks and dressers, then emptied on the floor; even all the fancy carpets had been pulled back, as if the men were searching for secret hiding places.

Fargo stepped into the study and felt a jolt of shock. Mitt Brennan was seated in a fancy wing chair.

Fargo's hand dropped to the butt of his Colt. He had challenged the man in the chair twice before he realized he was dead.

But it wasn't the wound to Brennan's side, sustained earlier during the attack, that had killed him. It was the neat bullet hole in the back of his skull. Brennan had been shot from behind while he was sitting, and Fargo didn't need a Philadelphia lawyer to tell him who did it or why. Brennan was no use to Hollis Blackburn hurt—so Hollis, true to his nature, simply murdered him.

An open wall safe told the rest of the story. Hollis had taken whatever gold he managed to steal and was even now fleeing from the Black Hills.

But Fargo had a memory he couldn't shake: the memory of a dying man, suffering horribly with mountain fever and surrounded by his dead comrades. Men tossed into the underbrush like so many empty bottles—and all because of the orders of a greedy, arrogant, cowardly man who even now was headed someplace else to do it all over again.

"It won't stand," Fargo said aloud to the empty room. "I won't let it."

Then he left to track down Hollis Blackburn.

15

"I'm going with you, Fargo."

Fargo, busy stuffing two days worth of trail rations into a saddle-bag, glanced up at Philly Tyler. The short-legged grifter was climbing awkwardly over the top pole of the corral to join Fargo.

"Going with me where?" he asked.

"Don't play it coy, tough fellow, that's for the ladies. You rode over to the Alliance this morning in hopes of confronting Hollis Blackburn. He wasn't there, which I could have told you. Hollis has a real knack for the well-timed strategic withdrawal. So now you're going to trail him. And I'm going with you."

"I'm a one-man outfit," Fargo replied as he filled another saddlebag with oats for his Ovaro. Grass was lush hereabouts, but there would be no time for grazing. The folks in Busted Hump were still up against it, and Fargo had no intention of staying gone very long.

"I've already figured that out about you," Philly said. "But loner or no, I'm asking you to make an exception for me. I have rights in this matter, Fargo."

"You keep saying that. But what are these rights?"

Philly's eyes drilled into him like bullets. "Do *you* spill your guts, Fargo, about everything that happened in your past?"

Fargo matched his stare. "I take your point, Philly. But I also don't drag other people into settling my old scores for me. And even if I did, I'd figure they had a right to know the facts."

"Ahh, look, Fargo—I know a man can't always stand up for his honor or he'd never stop fighting. Hell, I swallow insults every day, and now and then some drunk bully cleans my plow just for the exercise. I don't lose sleep over it, that's just the cost of doing business. But there's some things that can't be let go. In fact, things so important a man is a scoundrel if he doesn't balance the ledger."

Fargo gazed at this odd little moon-faced man with the mutton-chop whiskers and embroidered batwing chaps. He happened to agree with what Philly had just said. In fact, "balancing the ledger" was why Fargo himself was doing this. Until real law finally came to the Black Hills, there had to at least be justice.

"Why, Philly?" he demanded. "Why are you so het up about killing Hollis Blackburn?"

"Why are *you*, Fargo? You don't know the man from Adam, never even met him. Yet, here you go again, braving danger in the interest of seeing good prevail. Not one damn thing in it for you that I can see. Why, Fargo? Especially when—let's face it—the very people you're helping are fortune seekers themselves."

The Trailsman was silent for a few moments while he checked his cinches.

"Several reasons," he finally replied. "But one sticks out in memory right now: that dying prospector I talked to a few days ago. Never mind if he was a fortune seeker or not, I don't deny any man his dream. The point is, he was laying there in terrible misery, Philly. Only moments away from dying. Hurt, scared, prob'ly missing his family. But you know what he was worried about? He was worried I'd get too close and get infected. Even begged me not to bury them so's I wouldn't be at risk. Now I ask you, old son: How does a man like that, poor as Job's turkey, stack up against a man of high birth like Hollis Blackburn?"

Philly nodded. "My point exactly. Only, in my case, it's much more personal. Please, Fargo? I have rights in this matter, I swear I do. This time it's not a con game."

Fargo couldn't deny the intensity of Philly's emotions, which spoke volumes. He did appear to have certain rights in this matter even if he wouldn't divulge his particular grievance against Hollis. But Philly Tyler hardly impressed him as a man well-versed in trailcraft.

"Philly, even a justified desire for vengeance ain't worth spit if a man can't back it up. You see all them smoke signals off to the east? It may be true that we've eliminated the danger from the Alliance. But now we got even bigger problems—a full-bore Sioux uprising. That's the straight, old son. You need to worry about getting the hell out of here with your hair still in place. Leave Hollis Blackburn to me."

"*No*, damnit! If you don't take me, Fargo, I'll . . . damnit-all, I'll follow you! I've *got* to be there when you catch up to Hollis. It means more to me than life itself."

Fargo sighed. He had no trouble laying down the law to others in clear-cut matters of leadership. The problem was, he deeply respected whatever was felt deeply in another man's heart. Evidently, Philly really did have a powerful personal stake in all this—rights Fargo felt bound to respect despite his misgivings.

"Can you even ride?" he demanded.

"You kidding?" Philly slapped his gaudy chaps. "These aren't just for show. Us city slicks have horses around, too, you know."

"Uh-hunh. Dray nags." Skye pointed with his chin in the direction of the claybank gelding. "Pow rode that one earlier, he's still tacked and ready to ride. Get horsed and take a few turns around the corral for me."

"Wouldja look at that?" Philly scoffed as he approached the claybank. "That clumsy Pow left a stirrup stuck on the saddle horn. *There's* your tenderfoot."

Philly unhooked the stirrup so it dangled again, stepped into it as he grabbed the horn, then promptly smashed face-down into the dirt as the saddle slid completely around and crashed down on top of him.

Despite the pressing matters on his mind, Fargo laughed so hard he had to bend forward and grip his knees.

"Philly, you cap the climax. All them city horses you bragged on must be pulling cabbage wagons, not wearing saddles. Pow deliberately left the stirrup on the saddle horn to remind himself, or another rider, that the girth was loose. That's the custom and any real horsebacker would know it."

Philly, looking sheepish, shook the saddle off his back and stood up, dusting himself off.

"All right, I didn't know that about the stirrup," he confessed. "But I can ride. Watch."

Philly grabbed the saddle rig, swung it a few times to build momentum, then tossed it onto the claybank and deftly cinched the girth. The stirrups were adjusted too long for his legs, but he managed to swing aboard. He shook out the reins and thumped his heels against the gelding. He trotted it around the corral, guiding the horse well through several sharp turns with the reins.

"You ain't the worse rider," Fargo conceded. "And that's excellent horseflesh, so take the claybank. You can go with me, Philly. But just remember—I warned you not to. Good chance you'll get yourself killed. And a flint arrow point makes for a hard, painful death. They like to shoot low in the guts, so it takes days to bleed out."

Fargo glanced around the camp. Many were packing up their belongings. "I'd rather see you do what the rest are—leave the Black Hills, and pronto. But you're set on going with me, I can see that. I'll have to shoot you to stop you. So get what you need, I'm leaving in a few minutes."

"You're straight goods, Fargo. Thanks."

"I'm in charge," Fargo added, aiming a level stare at the city dude. "You're just riding along, all right? No tricks up your sleeve?"

"Sure. Understood. Just riding along. That's all I ask."

"Uh-huh," Fargo said again, already wondering if this was a mistake.

Earlier, Fargo had cut sign on Hollis Blackburn and knew he was driving a four-wheeled conveyance of some sort behind a two-horse team. Judging from the depths of the wheel ruts, he was making off with something heavy—and gold seemed the most likely cargo.

It was well into the afternoon when Fargo and Philly

Tyler rode out, bearing northeast toward the Belle Fourche River. For some time Hollis followed an old stage road plagued by washouts and rockslides.

"My opinion of Hollis has gone up a little," Fargo admitted. "He's a determined man and a damn sharp driver."

After perhaps two hours of steady riding, they emerged from the Black Hills onto the surrounding Dakota plains.

"Now my opinion of him has gone back down, that damn fool," Fargo muttered.

He pointed out toward the humped silhouette of a butte rising into the sky. Even now black signal smoke rose against a dome of bottomless blue.

"That's Bear Butte," he said. "The area is crawling with Sioux. Sort of a staging area for the attacks into the Black Hills. But so far Hollis is bearing right down on 'em."

"Only one logical reason why," Philly opined. "He's meeting a boat at Bridger's Landing on the Belle Fourche. There's no other way out from here. Indians have shut down all the stage service."

"Bridger's Landing," Fargo repeated. "That's right. Use to be a trading post there near a big gravel bar where flatboats can pull in easy."

Philly nodded. "There's an old salt named Nolichucky Jack, owns a flatboat. He rents his boat out, hauls passengers and cargo to the railhead at Elk Springs. It costs dear, but he's the only passenger service in the area."

"And to get to Bridger's Landing," Fargo recalled, "you have to pass Bear Butte."

Philly nodded. "Hollis isn't stupid, he'll try to swing around them. He knows how dangerous traveling in this direction is. He has to be mighty desperate to escape from somebody. And I'd say that somebody is you, Fargo."

"Maybe. But he's so desperate he's got stupid. 'Swing wide' of the Sioux? They'll spot his dust from miles out—prob'ly already have. And given the mood they're in these days, his scalp will end up in a cape. Matter fact. . . ."

Fargo sent a cross-shoulder glance in the direction of the sun. Only about an hour and a half or so before it would set. Fargo, who'd been up the night before supervising defenses, was still running a serious sleep deficit.

"No sense raising dust puffs in daylight ourselves," he decided. "Hollis, if he's still free, can't be making very good ime in that weighted-down rig. And I can't see him getting past the Sioux, anyhow. Let's turn in and rest until dark. This is open country, and the sky is clear—won't be bad or night riding."

Fargo led them into a swale between two low sand ridges. Their mounts were well-grained and had just tanked up at he last creek. So the two men stripped the horses down to he neck leather and quickly dried the sweat from them with handfuls of grass.

Fargo cleared himself a little wallow, using his saddle for a pillow. He slanted his hat over his face to block out the westering sun.

"How'd a smart fellow like you," he asked Philly as he waited for sleep to claim him, "end up a grifter in this part of the frontier? The Sioux and the Cheyenne are still far from tamed—no boys to mess with."

Philly chuckled. "Would you believe I once dreamed of being a famous saddle maker in Saint Louis? My father owned a harness shop in Philadelphia, taught me how to work leather. But somewhere along the line I developed a lair for crimping cards and bilking the rubes."

"That explains your choice of profession," Fargo told him, "but not why you choose to practice it here. It's because this is where Hollis Blackburn is, right? You trailed him here. Matter fact, it's the only reason you even came here."

"I thought you wanted some sleep?" Philly reminded him, ignoring the question. "I thought you strong frontier types were also men of few words?"

"Done jawing," Fargo mumbled, and moments later he was asleep.

Fargo's infallible inner sentry roused him just after sunset. Philly, however, woke up slower. Fargo had to shake him good before he managed to stand up and saddle his horse.

"Hold up a minute," Fargo said when Philly was mounted and ready to ride. The Ovaro's ears were pricked forward in a way the Trailsman had learned to heed. The claybank, too, kept raising its head to sample the air.

He moved cautiously up onto the nearest ridge, his gaze aimed toward the blue-black night sky in the east, toward

Bear Butte. He could see nothing distorting the horizon line. But Fargo listened intently until he heard it: the hollow thud of riders, many riders. They were approaching fast on unshod horses.

"It's Sioux," he reported to Philly. "War party, most likely. Only a war party will ride at night."

"You think they're heading into the Black Hills?" Philly asked.

Fargo nodded. "They want to be in place for a sunrise strike."

"Busted Hump?" Philly added, worry spiking his tone.

"Distinct possibility. Or the Alliance, or maybe even the town of Shoshone Falls. With all the bluecoats gone fighting Mormons, they got their pick."

"Folks in Busted Hump are just getting over a fever epidemic," Philly fretted. "Then this morning they fought off that attack Hollis sicced on them. But without you to organize them, they'll not whip the Sioux. Besides, they won't be ready for it."

"I got faith in Elijah and Pow, they're natural leaders. Just hope it ain't Busted Hump that's being attacked," Fargo advised him. "Because, believe me, even though I plan on getting back there fast, my being there won't save them. Not from seven bands of the best horse warriors in the world."

"Speaking of which . . . what do *we* do?" Philly asked nervously. "Right now, I mean?"

"Nothing until they ride past. We're low enough here they won't spot us—not at the speed they're traveling. Light down and hobble your horse."

Both men tied their mounts foreleg to rear with rawhide strips. The war party had moved close enough now that Fargo could feel vibrations through the soles of his boots.

"I don't like this," he said, peering out over the lip of the ridge. "They're cutting it closer to our position than I thought. We best back up a hundred yards or so."

They knocked off the hobbles, hit leather, and wheeled their horses to retreat. That's when disaster struck.

Fargo heard a sudden, buzzing rattle behind him, and that's all it took to spook the claybank Philly rode. The gelding reared up, then spun around and bolted out onto the open flats, Philly screaming blue murder.

Fargo cursed, knowing the grifter lacked the horse-manship skills to get his mount under control in time. And as luck would have it, the spooked horse was galloping headlong into the attack.

Fargo watched it all unfold, helpless to intervene. Rescuing Philly right now was out of the question—he had already been spotted in the generous moonlight. In moments he would be their prisoner.

Fargo knew that if he showed himself now, they'd simply both be killed or captured. His best bet—and Philly's—was to lay low and hope the Sioux were in too big a hurry to waste time poking around this area for more whiteskins. He didn't think they'd kill Philly—not right away, anyhow. When the Sioux took captives, their fate generally had to be discussed at council.

Philly had finally managed to rein in the claybank, but he was immediately swarmed by warriors. Fargo winced when one of them swung a wooden war club into Philly's skull, knocking him out cold—if not worse. He was lashed into the saddle with his ankles roped together under the horse's belly.

Fargo watched as the war party (he estimated them at about a hundred braves) now subdivided into groups of ten, heading out in different directions but generally bearing southwest into the Black Hills. He knew it was a favorite Indian strategy to avoid detection; they would rendezvous as one body just before the attack.

Fargo kept his eye on the group holding Philly. When they had a brief lead on him, he kicked the Ovaro forward, following them. He wasn't sure what his options were, if any. But he knew he'd better create one, and soon.

One finally did occur to him, although it was reckless enough to call suicidal. Yet, it was inspired by Philly's little lecture on distractions as a key element in trickery. And it was Philly's thinking, after all, that got Fargo past the Alliance bloodhounds. Maybe it would work again.

After about an hour of steady loping, the braves halted their half-wild mustangs at a little creek among some low, grassy hills. Philly was groggy, but conscious, and since he couldn't use hands or feet to control his horse, his captors simply left him in the saddle and ignored him.

Fargo, halted about a hundred yards behind them, led

the Ovaro on foot into some tangled growth near the creek. He left the reins dangling and, keeping a low hill between himself and the braves, hooked around to a grassy hollow just south of them.

He pulled a phosphor from the pouch on his belt, along with some crumbled bark he always carried for kindling. Fargo quickly pulled bunches of grass, piled it over the kindling, and snapped the match to life with his thumb. Seconds later his little fire was sparking and smoking.

Now he had to move fast—it wouldn't be long before that fire caught the braves' attention. He sprinted back to the Ovaro, then led him forward as close to Philly as he dared, waiting.

The wind gusted, a tongue of flame licked out into view above the low hill, and a warrior shouted excitedly, pointing toward the growing grass fire.

As Fargo had hoped, all of the braves ran to investigate. He sprang forward, cut Philly's hands and feet loose, then prepared to mount.

"Fargo! Timely met," Philly greeted him, though in a weakened, somewhat slurred voice. "Let's haul!"

"Wait!"

"Are you loco, man? Those red sons have already split my head open."

But Fargo had just noticed all the cockleburs clinging to the legs of his buckskin trousers. He knew he'd play hell trying to outrun Indian ponies—the Sioux were partial to slitting their horses's nostrils for extra wind and endurance. But another distraction just might give them the head start they badly needed. . . .

He shot a glance over his shoulder. The suspicious braves were smothering the fire. He raced from pony to pony, placing a few burrs under the pad of each buffalo-hide saddle.

"Fargo!" Philly hissed desperately. "Oh, Mother Mary! They *see* you!"

"Raise dust!" Fargo shouted even as he made a flying leap and vaulted himself over the Ovaro's rump and into the saddle.

Behind them, yipping war cries broke out. Some of the Sioux had taken their weapons with them when they ran to investigate the fire. Fargo heard the sharp, thin crack of old British trade guns, the twang and flutter of arrows being launched and zwipping past their ears.

He leaned low and forward to lower his target profile, then glanced over his shoulder. The first braves had leaped onto their ponies, driving those burrs in and infuriating their spirited mounts, several of which bucked off their surprised riders.

A grin eased his lips apart. But he knew their lead was slim and precarious. At this speed, a gopher hole could spell doom.

"Let that claybank stretch it out!" he shouted over to Philly even as he thumped his own heels harder into the Ovaro. "If we can open up enough of a lead, they'll give up. A Sioux figures, why push if a thing won't move? But if they do decide to run us to ground? Brother, you better pray that claybank's got plenty of bottom."

Fargo's hunch proved sound. Both horses, as if competing between themselves, ran strong, enjoying this romp. The Ovaro, though worked hard lately, had been cooped up in mountain canyons. He seemed eager to gallop across open flats, and the gelding kept stride. The Sioux apparently had bigger ambitions and decided to spare their ponies this reckless chase after two crazy whiteskins.

"Heap big doin's in the *Paha Sapa*," Fargo remarked when they stopped to let the horses blow. "Let's get this business over with and haul freight back to Busted Hump. The Sioux ain't likely to actually attack at night. We might get lucky, city slick, and arrive just in time for the opening of the ball."

"That's what you call luck, huh?" Philly smirked in the moonlight. His right eye was swollen nearly shut from the impact of the war club. "Now luck, to me, is when rich, gullible pilgrims arrive in town soon after I've salted a mine with fool's gold."

"Each to his own," Fargo said. "Don't be surprised, though, when one of those pilgrims *rock*-salts your sitter."

Fargo rode in a few wide loops, bent low in the saddle to study the ground. He whistled to Philly when he'd picked up Blackburn's track again.

"My hat's off to him again," Fargo admitted as Philly rode up. "Hollis played it smart, all right, and avoided that war party. Not by sheer luck, either. He knew just where to drive his team so he'd stay on course for Bridger's Landing, yet put hills between him and the Sioux. I do believe the man can star navigate."

"No surprise there," Philly said. "You ever notice how hard it is to kill a cockroach? Hollis Blackburn specializes in two things: causing the death of others, and saving his own worthless hide at any expense."

About an hour later both riders crested a ridge. Below them, the serpentine twists of the Belle Fourche River reflected like quicksilver in the moonlight.

"*Ho*-ly Hannah!" Philly exclaimed, pointing. "That's Bridger's Landing below—and *look*!"

But Fargo didn't require help seeing it. A flatboat—or what remained of one—was moored to a stanchion near a long gravel spit. Obviously it had been burning for some time. Most of the wooden boat was now just charred wreckage; spikes of flame still shot into the sky from portions that remained ablaze.

"C'mon," Fargo said, kicking the Ovaro forward after a close scrutiny of the area.

But the men were too late to help the boat's skipper and crew. Fargo and Philly found them scattered along the shore of the river, dead. All had been scalped and mutilated.

Philly quickly turned away, retching. "Is that what I *think* it is stuffed into their mouths?" he asked.

"Yep. That's what they do with it after they castrate them."

"That's Nolichucky Jack," Philly said grimly, pointing toward a bearded corpse. "Or it was. You think they got Hollis, too? I don't see his body anywhere. Nor his mistress, either."

"If they've been captured, where's their conveyance?" Fargo asked, glancing all around. "But the track comes down this way. Hold on a minute."

Fargo backtracked until he had spotted the rutted trail of Blackburn's rig. Both men followed it toward the river. Then it suddenly veered toward a marsh.

"Now I see what happened," Fargo muttered in a hushed voice. "The attack on the flatboat must have commenced while Hollis was approaching. So he drove into the marsh to hide. It was that or die."

"Think he's still in there?" Philly asked.

"That ground is like soup. If he drove in there, I'll guaran-damntee he didn't drive back out. Hobble your mount, Philly."

Both men advanced on foot into the marsh. Their feet made spongy, sucking sounds in the stewlike muck.

"There," Fargo whispered, pointing off to the right.

Generous moonwash revealed an eerie sight. A loaded buckboard had sunk up to its hubs in the soupy mess. The team had been unhitched, but horses hated being forced to stand in wet ground, and now both animals were hopelessly tangled in their picket ropes, exhausted from the struggle to free themselves. A man in a well-tailored suit sat on the board seat, waving gloved hands, talking to the pretty woman beside him.

". . . *told* you to stop that goddamn bloody screaming, didn't I, luv? Those Indians could have heard you. . . ."

"That's Hollis," Philly confirmed in a whisper. A strange sheen came over the little man's eyes.

But Fargo had no time to wonder about it. He had just realized something, and a powerful chill moved up his spine: the woman slumped beside Hollis Blackburn was dead. And judging from the way her swollen tongue protruded, she'd been strangled.

"Yet another woman he's killed," Philly whispered.

Fargo wondered about that remark, but this was no time for questions. He shucked out his Colt and both men crept forward. Oddly, Hollis hardly even reacted when the muzzle of Fargo's gun kissed his temple. The Englishman glanced at him with resigned eyes.

"So you've come for me at last," Hollis announced in a business-as-usual voice. "The legendary Skye Fargo, the agent of my final reckoning. I've been expecting this moment, Fargo. It was destined. Predestined, actually. Somehow the Fates decided to cast you as my executioner."

Fargo glanced into the back of the buckboard. Several leather valises were stuffed full.

"Gold, I take it," he said.

Hollis nodded. He sent an indifferent glance toward

Philly, but had never seen the odd-looking little man before and dismissed him. His full attention went back to Fargo.

"Yes, gold," he replied. "The stuff that dreams are made of. I'd offer to share it with you, Fargo, but I know that's pointless. Men like you are beyond the normal temptations."

"Maybe Fargo is, Mr. Blackburn, but *I'm* not."

Startled, both Hollis and Fargo looked at Philly. He had the drop on Fargo with a little five-shot Colt pocket model. Little in frame, but not in bore.

"Drop your pistol *now*, Fargo," Philly ordered in a cold, no-nonsense voice. "Or I swear by all things holy, I'll burn you down!"

16

Fargo, confused by the sudden and unexpected twist in this trail, was slow to react to the command. The Colt leaped in Philly's fist, and several fringes were ripped from the left arm of Fargo's buckskin shirt.

"That was just a crease. I said *drop* it, Fargo, or the next one gets drilled right through your stubborn head. You've seen me work sleight of hand tricks—I'm *good* with this, so don't push me."

This time Fargo decided to obey, not liking the crazy sheen that had taken over Philly's eyes—the dangerous sheen of an obsessed man at the end of his long mission. He flipped his gun off to the side.

Hollis, whose face had been a mask of defeated resignation seconds earlier, suddenly looked like a man who'd just struck a lode while burying garbage. He stared at the odd, moon-faced little stranger with new curiosity.

"If your object is to steal this gold, sir," Hollis told Philly, "I'll not resist. But I strongly advise you to kill Fargo *now*. He's too crafty to let live, and every second you delay gives him time to react. Believe me, he'll never let you escape."

"Oh, I'll kill him, all right," Philly said smugly. "But I

don't intend to steal your gold, Mr. Blackburn. I'm hoping to join forces with you."

It was difficult to tell who looked more mule-kicked by this announcement: Hollis or Fargo.

"Join forces?" Hollis repeated woodenly. "Have we even met, sir?"

Philly shook his head. "You're not an easy man to approach, Mr. Blackburn. They call me Philly Tyler. I've been hearing about you for months now. How you're the big wheel and everybody else is just a cog. In other words, a man of power and vision—the kind of man who'd appreciate my talents."

Blackburn nodded, a self-satisfied smile easing his lips apart. He swallowed Philly's flattery without effort. "I appreciate them already, stout lad," he assured Philly.

"But then along comes Fargo here, playing the big he bear, bragging how he's going to clean up the trash in the Black Hills, starting with you. So I pretended to throw in with him, knowing the arrogant rube would lead me to you."

By now Hollis looked like a condemned man who'd been granted a pardon one minute before the trap door was to open. He coldly shoved the murdered body of his mistress aside and climbed down off the seat.

"Well then . . . Philly, is it? This *is* a strange twist of fate," he said. "It so happens I do have an opening for a capable American assistant. And clearly you *are* capable. Quite bright, too, I saw that immediately in you. You help me get this gold to safety and we'll share it as full partners. With much more to be made later. As for you, Fargo. . . ."

One hand snaked inside his fancy, satin-faced coat and emerged clutching the Belgian pinfire revolver.

"What delicious irony!" he exclaimed. "Fickle Fate seems to've struck again. For the past few days I've been practically paralyzed with terror. Convinced you were sent by the hand of destiny to deal me my final reckoning. When all this time it was *you*, Fargo, that fate intended to blot out. This time, 'noble knight,' the despicable dragon wins."

His thumb reached up to cock the hammer back with a menacing click.

"Hold off a second, Mr. Blackburn," Philly called out. "I have a request. As a reward for pulling your bacon out of the fire, I want the pleasure of killing Fargo. He's made a fool of me every chance he could. Even made a public point of flagrantly bedding Mary Ellen, the woman I love. It would mean a lot to me if *I* could send this 'big man' under."

Hollis nodded, letting the hammer back down and holstering his weapon. "Fair enough, Philly. After all, I have no *personal* grudge against Mr. Fargo. He's comported himself like quite the gentleman since his arrival. Well—on with it, man! Kill him."

"I will, just let me savor the moment."

Fargo's first response, when Philly got the drop on him, was one of bitter betrayal. He recalled Philly's assurance from earlier, when he'd begged to go along: *This time it's not a con game.*

But by now Fargo had reminded himself that Philly was *always* working another con. I said I'd play this game through, he told himself, and I will. You don't tell a man you trust him unless you mean it.

"Well, my good man?" Hollis urged his new partner. "We have much to do and time is pressing. Look lively, fellow! 'Tis well 'twere done quickly, and all that. Squeeze that trigger."

Philly nodded toward Suzette's body, an admiring smile on his face. "What happened to her?"

Hollis lost his impatience for a moment and smiled as he looked at her in the ghostly moonlight. To Fargo, he looked proud of his sickness, like a great artist who had created something worthy. He twirled one end of his neat mustache.

"Female hysterics," he replied. "I warned her to stop screaming or the Sioux would find us. But the obstinate little thing panicked, I suppose, wouldn't listen."

"You could have just knocked her out," Fargo said.

"Why bother?" Philly demanded. "To a man with a pair on him, a man of real ambition, women are expendable. Like cigars. When they're used up, you toss them."

"Oh, we *will* thrive together, lad," Hollis said on a laugh. "Great minds think alike and that sort of thing. Besides, it's always wise to kill a concubine when you're tired of her. They know too much about your . . . business dealings."

"Same's true for young girls when you rape them," Philly

said, his tone tightening a little. "Right? Kill them after? 'Stone them into silence,' as the Kiowa put it?"

Fargo watched a glint of uncertainty enter Blackburn's eyes. "Yes, they, too. Let's get on with it, Philly, we can chat each other up later. Squeeze that trigger, man!"

"Reason I know you have a taste for young girls," Philly persisted, "is because I learned that about you when we were neighbors in Philadelphia."

Hollis started. *"We* were neighbors?"

Philly nodded. "About four years ago. Not quite neighbors, actually—my people weren't welcome in your part of town except to labor for you."

"We never met?"

Philly shook his head. "No. But you knew my little sister."

Here it is at last, Fargo realized, watching the Englishman's face drain white as if he'd been leeched.

"Tyler," Hollis repeated. "Of course . . . Hiram Tyler."

"Which is why I took the name Philly as I closed in on you. *Don't* do it," Philly snapped when Blackburn reached for his pinfire. "Yes, Hollis, Hiram Tyler. Rebecca was my little sister. You never met me, but I was the reason you suddenly took 'the geographical cure' as they say. You fled from Philadelphia and headed west to save your hide."

Philly looked at Fargo. "Sorry for the drop play, Skye. But I know you. You wouldn't have killed Hollis unless he resisted, and he was too scared to fight you. You would've hauled him off to the law someplace."

Fargo nodded. "Prob'ly, all the time praying he'd make a break for it so I could cut him down and save the hanging bill. But then, I ain't heard your side of it."

"I'm not usually strong enough to tell it," Philly admitted. "That's why I went through that little act just now, to show you how sick and evil this piece of shit really is. Becky was only fourteen then, Skye, the sweetest, prettiest, most innocent girl you ever saw. The kind of girl you'd call the essence of grace and goodness. After consumption took our father, Becky and I both took jobs to support ourselves and our mother."

"Muh-Mister Tyler," Hollis cut in, stammering, "you—"

"Shut your filthy sewer of a mouth," Philly cut him off. He looked at Fargo again.

"Hollis had himself a fancy house on Market Street. He hired Becky as a daily servant. Several weeks later, Becky turns up dead in a back alley, gutted like a fish. No clues, the police claimed, and since she wasn't rich like Hollis here, who cared?"

"Mr. Tyler," Hollis tried again, "there was no evidence presented at court. . . ."

Hollis fell silent when Philly produced a leather-bound diary from a coat pocket. "No evidence the police would accept, you mean, after you paid them off. But Becky kept this diary, Skye. Hollis had repeatedly raped her. The last entry, the night before she was killed, explains that she confronted him with a threat to go to the law. So he eliminated her."

Philly nodded toward the dead woman slumped over the seat of the buckboard. "Just like he eliminated her. A cigar butt ground under his heel. . . ."

Philly choked up, so Fargo finished the story for him. "And you've just been biding your time, right? Trailing him, waiting for this kind of chance."

Philly nodded. "That's why I can't let you pick your gun up just yet, Skye. Never come between a dog and his meat—*this* son of the Union Jack is mine."

"Can't say's I blame you, Philly. Just keep one thing in mind: you don't want to sink to his level. However you handle this, you've got to square with it for the rest of your life."

"Oh, I've already come to that conclusion myself," Philly assured him. "You notice I haven't taken his gun? Skye, I have no legal right to execute him. But I can legally challenge him to a gun fight under territorial law, right?"

Fargo nodded. "Yep. Now if you two gents will excuse me, I need to answer the call of nature."

Fargo turned and started strolling off into the trees.

"Fargo!" Hollis shouted. "Don't leave me alone with him!"

"You'll have fair odds. It's more of a chance than you gave his sister," Fargo said without turning round. "Or them prospectors you infected. Kind of ironic, ain't it, Hollis? You named the wrong man as the agent of your 'final reckoning.' "

Fargo never once doubted the outcome of the gun duel—

Philly had a magician's hands, and a powerful will to settle accounts. But Fargo had been forced to witness enough death in his lifetime. Given the choice, he'd rather not see it.

He heard the sound of Hollis begging; a long silence; then a single, almost insignificant gun shot. A minute later Philly joined him, looking none too happy.

"I killed him clean with one shot to the brain," he said, his tone showing his disgust with himself. "After the *hell* he put Becky through, I should've at least shot him low in the guts, made him suffer."

"Will you listen to your own bunk?" Fargo scoffed. "You're apologizing for not being as low as Blackburn. That's the whole point about proper law and order, Philly— no man can place himself above it. Just look at it this way: all his life Hollis Blackburn gave a short measure and a long price. Now, thanks to you, he's paid up himself—paid in full."

Fargo guided Philly toward their nearby horses. "We're taking that gold," he said. "The Alliance or whoever they are had no right to dispossess the prospectors. So that gold will be divvied up equally among all the residents of Busted Hump. Compensation for what they suffered and lost."

Fargo paused. "I'd like to bury the woman, at least," he told Philly. "I don't judge a gal by the male company she keeps. But there just ain't time, and I'd rather help the living. If we ride hard, we *might* get back to the Black Hills before those Sioux attack."

Fargo freed Blackburn's team horses, but they were too exhausted for service, so all he could do was turn them out to graze and rest in the surrounding grass. He and Philly each tied a gold-filled valise to their saddles and pointed their bridles west toward the looming mass of the Black Hills.

For the rest of that night they pounded their saddles hard. Toward dawn it rained, just enough to settle the dust. The men had paused briefly, on the crest of a low rise, to let the horses blow.

Philly spoke up. "Nothing will ever bring Becky back, Skye. And I'm not trying to play God. That's the first time I ever killed anyone, and I hope I never have to do it again.

It's a sickening feeling. But I'll sleep better now knowing that monster has killed his last innocent human being."

Fargo nodded. "You'll be all right. Sometimes a broken bone heals stronger. You killed a man who required killing. You handled it right, now put it behind you."

In silent accord both men glanced back toward that fateful spot. The land was level and clear behind them for miles, and the eastern sky was now flaming into light—enough light to reveal the dark specks of carrion birds circling over the Belle Fourche River.

"Looks like the Vulture God will finally be meeting some of his flock," Fargo remarked. "C'mon—let's dust our hocks."

He had predicted they could reach the Black Hills by sunrise, and he was right. But even as they entered the northern tip, riding south of Elk Horn Peak, Fargo realized the Sioux had struck early.

"That ain't signal smoke," he said grimly, pointing south toward Busted Hump. Huge black columns of smoke rose into the early morning sky.

"If that's Busted Hump," Philly replied, "we're too damn late."

But it wasn't Busted Hump—not quite yet, anyway. That was confirmed an hour later when the two exhausted riders reached the camp and found it untouched.

"They've destroyed the Alliance property," reported a worried Elijah Stone. "Been raising holy hell there since before sunup. Why couldn't they've held off a day or two? Hell, most of us already started packing to clear out of here."

"Most of the miners cleared out yesterday," Pow added. "But I used Doc Boone's horse and sneaked over for a quick peek. A few of those fool miners musta stayed behind to loot the place. The Sioux caught them. I watched them skin one man alive. They buried another up to his neck and then sliced his eyelids off so the sun will fry his brain. They ain't showing no mercy, Mr. Fargo, and I got me a God fear we're next. Over a hunnert braves, and they're all wound up to a fare-thee-well."

"We're next," Fargo agreed. "And despite the long odds, we have to be ready to fight. We'll form up in three groups like we did for the attack yesterday. But that don't mean we *will* fight."

Fargo slanted a sly glance toward Philly as he said this. Doc Boone, along with Colleen, was among the crowd gathered around the two men. So was Mary Ellen Guidry, who had turned sideways to made sure he got a good view of her bursting bodice.

"Dang-garn-it, Fargo, there you go again," Doc Boone carped. "Talking in those confounded riddles. Them Injuns plan to deal us a world of misery, and you know it. We were already told as much by that flea-infested savage, what's-his-name, Winter Bear."

"True," Fargo replied, still aiming a thoughtful stare at Philly. "But the red man is a highly notional creature. And just maybe we can change their minds."

"Why you looking at me that way?" Philly demanded.

Fargo grinned. "Run along inside that 'spa' of yours, city boy, and put on your best coat—the one loaded with the most flashy tricks."

"Fargo, have you been grazing peyote? I'll do no such damn fool thing! These Sioux scare the snot outta me."

"This is pitiful." Fargo shook his head as if he couldn't believe what a little school girl Philly was being. "*You're* the one bragged to me how you did magic tricks for royalty and such. I see now it was all swamp gas."

"Like hell it was!" Philly spun on his heel and headed purposefully toward his gaudy shack. "All right then, Trailsman. You want a show, you'll get one. I'll no doubt lose my hair, but so what? You'll eat back your words."

"The Sioux are keen on magic and such," Fargo assured him. "Just go along with whatever I say. Keep your fear in your belly, not your face. Don't forget—if you lose *your* scalp, that means they're after mine, too. Knowing the Sioux, they'll want to take my beard right along with it. So you might say, for me, it's a matter of . . . saving face."

"If that's a joke," Philly called back from the door of his shack, "remind me to laugh later. Right now I'm too scared."

"It ain't a joke," Fargo promised. "It's a warning: you damn well better do just like I told you, or we'll be feeding worms."

17

A sentry in a tall pine, at the brim of Spearfish Canyon, called out the warning about an hour after sun-up: "Injuns comin'! About two miles off. Look to your weapons!"

"Let's go, white shaman," Fargo said, half dragging Philly up the slope with him. "I said get that scared look out of your face, hear me?"

Fargo slapped him a few times.

"Hey!" Philly protested. "I *heard* you! That wasn't necessary."

"I know. I'm just puttin' some color in your cheeks. Now you look like you got some blood in you."

"*Please* don't use that word right now."

Fargo was unarmed and carried a sharpened pole with a scrap of white cloth tied to it. He stopped about halfway up the steep slope and rammed the truce pole into the ground. He had no idea if the Sioux would honor it or not. But in his experience, Indians loved to be entertained and had great curiosity—and Philly presented a curious sight indeed in his feathered dude hat, frock coat with its hidden inner pockets, and bat-wing chaps.

"Oh, sainted backsides, here they come," he moaned, though Fargo noticed how the actor in him had taken over. Philly looked calm and confident, even a bit cocky.

The Sioux did not foolishly charge en masse as the miners had done. In fact Fargo had never seen Indians do battle that way. They remained for some time above on the canyon lip, safe for the time being and just watching.

"I see Winter Bear," Fargo remarked. "And Kills in Water and his brother Smiles Plenty. And that tough buck leading them must be Spotted Tail—I can tell from his crooked coup stick and the eagle crest on his shield."

"I can't tell any of them apart under all that paint," Philly said. "Jesus, here they come, Skye!"

"Steady on, hear me? You're on the royal stage now, Philly. This is Sioux royalty. Knock 'em into the aisle."

Spotted Tail, surrounded by some of his best warriors, rode slowly down to where the two men stood. The woman translator rode on a mare behind them. She was called forward.

Spotted Tail spoke a string of angry words, now and then striking his bone breast plate with one fist for emphasis.

"You were warned to get out, hair face," the woman translated. "Winter Bear generously granted your freedom. You knew the worst hurt in the world was coming to this place. Yet, here you are. Are you crazy-by-thunder?"

Fargo shrugged. "Nothing I can do. This man with me is *wakan*, holy. *Wichasa wakan*, a medicine man. His medicine is great, and I dare not defy him when he tells me to stay."

Spotted Tail and his braves laughed even before the translation, understanding Fargo's Lakota words.

"This *wasichu* fool a medicine man?" Spotted Tail demanded. "I can pronounce myself to be an eagle, can I not? But then I must fly to prove it. Let us *see* this great medicine."

Philly started out simple, but immediately hooked his audience, with some lively and amazingly fast juggling tricks. He produced a seemingly endless number of brightly colored balls, and soon he was juggling all of them off his nose, chin, forehead, both elbows and knees—so many that no one could count them and a murmur of approval swept through the mounted warriors.

Philly next moved on to some impressive tricks of manual dexterity and sleight of hand. He walked a silver dollar across his knuckles, then (by smoothly palming it) made the same coin seem to disappear from under a cup. But when he "found" the coin again, pulling it out of Spotted Tail's ear, several braves loosed impressed whoops.

"This was amusing," Spotted Tail conceded grudgingly. "But we, too, have our sacred clowns. Where is the proof this man is *wakan*? That he works true magic, not just clever tricks."

"If you got an ace tucked up one of those sleeves, Philly," Fargo muttered, "it's time to play it."

Philly announced through the translator: "I can do some-

157

thing no Lakota medicine man can do. I can sing to a gun and make it fire without ever touching it."

Derisive laughter rippled through the braves.

"You," Philly said, pointing to a warrior with an old trade musket. "Place your gun in the grass. Point it so the ball will hurt no one."

The brave glanced at Spotted Tail, who nodded permission. He leaped down and put the musket on the ground. The rest of the braves, forgetting their battle dignity, crowded around for a good look.

Philly whipped a bright scarlet and gold paper fan out with his right hand and began brushing it along the musket's wide muzzle. But Fargo knew his method by now—this was a distraction to keep attention off his left hand. It seemed to be only casually resting on Philly's left knee as he squatted near the weapon.

But Fargo had to bite his lower lip to keep a straight face when he saw the little wafer-shaped magnifying lens hidden in the circle formed by Philly's thumb and index finger. He was focusing the hot sun's rays directly into the touch hole of the priming pan.

Meantime, Philly sang a medley of bawdy tunes about "Lu-lu Girl" while he worked.

" 'She has freckles on her butt I love her,' " he was warbling when the musket suddenly twitched on the ground as its powder load detonated with a startling roar.

The warriors made enough racket to wake snakes, beating their shields, whooping, one even torturing a few sputtering notes out of a stolen army bugle. Spotted Tail, too, was visibly impressed. He looked at Philly with new respect.

"*Pilamaya kola*. Thank you very much, friend. This was indeed a demonstration of your powerful medicine."

Spotted Tail barked a command, and one of his subchiefs filled a decorated deer-bone pipe with sacred tobacco. He handed it to Spotted Tail. Fargo lit it and the chief smoked once to each of the four directions of the wind.

"With this *chanunpa*, this holy pipe, in his hand," Spotted Tail said, "a man can speak only the truth. I say this now, and this place hears me: the Lakota will grant three sleeps during which these whiteskins have safe passage from the *Paha Sapa*. In exchange, this great *wakan wichasa* will come live with us as our honored guest. He will teach our medicine men the true shaman powers."

When the translator finished with this, Philly whirled toward Fargo. "Now just a damn minute here, Fargo!"

"You'll treat him well?" Fargo asked Spotted Tail.

"As we would a great chief."

"See there?" Fargo reasoned with Philly. "You'll be living high on the hog. And after these folks here in Busted Hump are safe, I'll wander back around and buy your freedom back with some trade goods."

"Not for all the tea in China, Fargo! *Me*, go live with the Si—"

"Careful with that word," Fargo warned.

"With the Lakota, I mean? It's out of the question, Fargo. *No!* Absolutely not, forget it, don't even dream—"

"As with any great chief," Spotted Tail added, "he would have his pick from among our unmarried young women."

Philly abruptly stopped protesting, a grin splitting his moon face. "*Any*thing to pour oil on troubled waters. And, Skye? I'm not as handsome as you, the ladies don't flock to me. *This* could be my own Black Hills gold mine. So you take your time getting back to check on me, hear? I just might decide to go to the blanket, as they say."

Fargo grinned. "Oh, once you get a gander at them Lakota beauties, I 'spect you'll be going to the blankets plenty."

"That show Philly put on this morning was a real corker," Elijah boomed out at dinner that evening. "And the effort won't be wasted. I've talked to everybody in camp. Now that the epidemic is over, everybody pulls stakes tomorrow. Most of us will be headed toward less hostile diggings farther west."

Fargo, busy dipping one of Dotty's famous soda biscuits into the pot liquor of a delicious stew, welcomed the news. That meant they'd all be well clear of the Black Hills by the time Spotted Tail's deadline arrived.

"What about the prisoner?" he asked. "Orrin Jones."

"He tried to escape while you were gone," Pow informed him tersely, leaving it at that. Fargo caught his drift—Jones was dead. Nor was he surprised. Jones was instrumental—twice—in trying to wipe out Busted Hump.

"I *still* can't believe it, though," Colleen repeated yet again, her tone sad and wistful. "Shoshone Falls a ghost town."

"Just be glad folks were wise enough to clear out before the Sioux burned it down," Doc Boone said around a mouthful of stew. "Hell, the town itself ain't no great loss."

"You're just too mean and prideful to say it," Colleen chastised him. "But thanks to Skye and these folks at Busted Hump, we'll be able to set up practice again in Rapid City. Not to mention replace our buggy and clothes and personal possessions. They didn't have to give us such a generous share of that gold. Nor offer to take us out of here with them."

"I am too grateful," Doc grumped, picking at his teeth. "I just don't slop over like some do."

"Bosh!" Dotty exclaimed, reaching past baby Sarah in her lap to place a hand on Jimmy's tow head. "No need to feel grateful to us. We owe you and your uncle everything, Colleen. And as for *you*, Skye Fargo. . . ."

Dotty was a tough, practical woman, but she'd been through hell and back lately. Despite her best efforts, tears of love and gratitude sprang from her eyes.

"Son," she told Jimmy, fighting to control her voice, "you just learn to walk tall and talk soft like Mr. Fargo. That way you'll shape up into a fine man."

"Elijah," Skye said, "would you bust me in the chops if I kiss this fine woman?"

"Once is all right," Elijah said. "She's already got you on her mind anyhow. Hell, I don't mind if you even slip her a little tongue—that'll get me more lovin' tonight."

" 'Lijah, you foul-mouthed lumberjack!" she exclaimed, hands too full to slap him.

A few minutes later, while Doc Boone was meditating in the privy out back, Colleen was able to whisper in Fargo's ear, "Just one more time, Skye, please? We're both leaving in the morning."

"I plan on wandering down to the bathing pool in about an hour," he told her. "Why'n't you wait ten minutes or so, then wander down yourself? We'll make it a sweet good-bye to remember."

Fargo was on his way to make that sweet memory when

a figure stepped out of Elijah's shack behind him. "Fargo, a word?"

It was Doc Boone, holding the remaining bottle of sipping whiskey Fargo had returned to him. He had difficulty meeting Fargo's eyes.

"I didn't want to say this in front of the others," he began awkwardly, "but—well, damnit, I *liked* the feeling of being a good doctor again."

Fargo's eyes widened when Boone emptied the contents of the bottle into the dirt.

"I don't s'poze," Doc Boone added, "that you're the *biggest* scoundrel God ever made."

"Coming from you, Doc, that's high praise."

"Ahh, kiss my ass, you young fool."

"Rot in hell, you old goat."

The two men grinned and shook hands. Fargo went on downslope to the creek. He'd waited until late enough to have the place to himself in the buttery moonlight.

He stripped, plunged shivering into the cool water, sudsed himself, rinsed. Fargo smiled when the expected hands encircled him from behind, one grasping for his manhood. Luscious tits prodded into his back.

"Dumplin', you just follow your instincts," he encouraged as her hand began stroking him harder. "Oh, yeah, you do what you gotta, Colleen."

"Col-*leen*? Skye Fargo, you low-down, chicken-humping, two-timing—"

Too late he recognized the hill-country twang of Mary Ellen Guidry. The hand encircling his manhood suddenly tightened into a death grip. Fargo yowled in pain, then yelped in astonishment as a second naked, nubile female—the real Colleen this time—leaped into the pool and smacked Mary Ellen a good one.

"Unhand him, you low-bred, hillbilly slut!" Colleen snarled.

"Why, you high-toned, whorish hussy! I'll claw your eyeballs right out your high-falutin' face!" Mary Ellen shrieked back.

Within moments the two angry firebrands had ended up in the mud along the bank, locked in mortal combat, punching, biting, pulling hair. The catfight soon drew every male in camp.

But Fargo wisely gathered up his clothes and, under cover of the excitement, slipped off toward the corral, deciding on an early start. He had learned a hard lesson long ago—once two women started fighting over the same man, the doomed soul had only two choices: either clear the hell out fast or blow his own brains out and at least die quick.

He tacked his grained and rested Ovaro and searched the night sky until he found the Polestar. Then Fargo swung up into leather and rode off into the black velvet folds of darkness, listening to the wind whistle its ancient secrets in the nooks, crannies, crevasses, and nameless graves of these mysterious hills.

LOOKING FORWARD!

**The following is the opening
section of the next novel in the exciting
Trailsman series from Signet:**

THE TRAILSMAN #266
SIX-GUN SCHOLAR

*Texas Hill Country, 1860—
Where evil men need a lesson in lead,
and the Trailsman does the teaching.*

The big man in buckskins pressed his back against the
adobe wall of the old mission. His lake-blue eyes searched
the shadows. He knew the men he looked for were out
here somewhere, in the darkness next to the Alamo.

A few minutes earlier, Skye Fargo had been enjoying a
drink in the bar of the Menger Hotel, a block away. Then
he had seen the young woman walk through the lobby and
out into the night. More importantly, he had seen the men
who followed her.

Every instinct Fargo had developed during a life lived
mostly on the edge of danger told him that trouble was
brewing. The three men who left the Menger less than a
minute after the young woman wore range clothes and had
the look of hardcases about them.

Acting on his instincts, Fargo had drained the last of the beer in the mug and set the empty mug on the long hardwood bar. Then he'd turned and joined the procession, slipping into the darkness on the trail of the three men.

As he leaned against the mission wall, he dropped his hand to the walnut grips of the Colt holstered on his hip and let his keen ears do the work. He heard the whisper of boot leather on paving stones, a hissed breath, a quick rush of feet.

Then a scream—short, scared, and cut off abruptly, probably by a callused hand clapped over the young woman's mouth.

Trouble, all right.

Fargo drew his gun as he whirled around the corner of the mission. He spotted several figures struggling in the shadows a dozen feet away. Leveling the Colt, he barked, "Hold it!"

One of the figures broke apart from the others and spun toward him. Colt flame bloomed in the night, licking out from the muzzle of a gun like an orange tongue.

Expecting as much, Fargo had already thrown himself aside. The revolver in his hand bucked against his palm as he fired. He aimed low, not wanting to kill unless he had to.

The man who had taken the shot at Fargo screamed and twisted half around as the slug ripped through his thigh. He toppled off his feet, his gun falling from his hand and skidding across the paving stones in front of the old chapel.

But there were still two more of them, and one grated, "Get that bastard, whoever he is!"

A second man leaped at Fargo, swinging his arm. This man wielded a knife instead of a gun. Not a normal knife, though. Fargo saw starlight wink off a long length of cold steel and realized that the man had a machete.

Dropping to a knee, Fargo used his Colt to parry the killing stroke. With a clang, the blade clashed with the gun barrel. Fargo thrust out a leg and used it to sweep his opponent's legs out from under him while he was still off balance.

The man fell heavily, landing hard on the ground with a pained grunt. Fargo reversed the revolver and struck out with it. The butt of the gun thudded against the man's skull.

That was one more out of the fight, at least for a few minutes, Fargo thought.

The woman screamed again. With only one man holding her now, she fought furiously to free herself from his grip. He cursed and slammed a fist against the side of her head.

Fargo saw the craven blow as he surged to his feet. He lunged toward the remaining enemy. The man shoved the woman hard, thrusting her right into Fargo's path.

"You want the bitch so much, take her!"

Fargo couldn't stop in time. He crashed into the woman. Their feet tangled together, and they both went down.

He managed to hold on to his gun and snapped a shot at the third man, driving him back. A few feet away, the second man struggled to shake off the effect of Fargo's blow and get back to his feet. He made it and stumbled toward the alley on the far side of the old mission.

"Come on, let's get out of here!" the third man said. Before he ran, though, he had one last thing to do.

The gun in his hand roared twice.

Fargo threw himself over the woman to shield her with his own body as the shots rang out. Then he realized the bullets hadn't been directed at them. The third man had fired at the first one, the one Fargo had wounded.

Fargo squeezed the Colt's trigger again as the third man darted around the corner into the alley. He knew his shot missed because he heard the slug whine off harmlessly into the night, ricocheting off something.

He pushed himself upright and dragged the young woman with him, his free hand firmly gripping her arm. "Get back to the hotel!" he told her and gave her a gentle push to get her started in that direction.

She gasped. "What about you?"

"I'm going after the other two," Fargo said.

He darted to the corner. The darkness in the alley was stygian, and the thought of venturing into it after two armed men would have been daunting to most people. Fargo's temper was up, though, and he hesitated only a moment before plunging into the shadows.

As he did so, he heard the swift rataplan of hoofbeats. He stopped and listened to the sound fade into the distance. His Ovaro was stabled a couple of blocks away, and by the time he could reach the magnificent black-and-white stallion, the two men would be gone.

Fargo's jaw tightened. He didn't have to like it, but he had to accept the fact that his opponents had gotten away from him.

He turned and walked back along the front of the chapel. When he reached the dark shape sprawled on the ground, he dropped to a knee and reached out to check for a pulse. There wasn't one, just as Fargo expected.

The third gunman had made sure that the wounded man wouldn't talk. Fargo dug a lucifer out of the pocket of his buckskin shirt and snapped the sulfur match into life with his thumbnail.

The dead man's shirtfront was sodden with blood from the two wounds in his chest. Considering the bad light in the plaza in front of the mission, that was good shooting, Fargo thought grimly.

He straightened, dropped the match, and ground it out with the toe of his boot. Turning south toward the hotel, he looked for the young woman he had rescued.

There was no sign of her.

Well, he *had* told her to get back to the hotel, he thought. If she had any sense, she had fled inside. Fargo walked toward the hotel, keeping his gun in his hand until he had almost reached the entrance. Then and only then did he holster the revolver.

The Menger Hotel, built of limestone with elaborate ironwork facades and window grilles, was the finest hotel in San Antonio and one of the finest west of the Mississippi. Only a year old, it had been built to be a showcase by W. A. Menger, the owner of a prosperous local brewery.

To Fargo it was a place to get a drink and a decent meal, and to sleep in a real bed for the first time in quite a while. He hadn't expected to run into trouble here, but he supposed he should have. After all, trouble seemed to follow him no matter where he went.

He had ridden in from the Big Bend country of West Texas, arriving in San Antonio just after dusk. After getting a room in the hotel, he'd stepped into the bar for a drink to cut the trail dust before going in search of something to eat. That was when he'd noticed the young woman and the three men following her.

Now his stomach reminded him that it had been a long time since he'd gnawed on the piece of jerky at midday. But there was still the question of what had happened to the woman.

Fargo went to the desk in the lobby and asked the clerk, "Did you see a woman come in here a couple of minutes ago?"

The man frowned in thought and shook his head. "No, I don't believe I did."

"She probably would have looked upset, maybe scared."

The clerk's frown deepened. "Oh, my goodness. Was there some sort of trouble outside? I thought I heard shooting a few minutes ago."

San Antonio might be a frontier town, but this fella was no frontiersman, Fargo thought. "If you didn't see her, it doesn't matter, does it?"

"If there's a problem, Mr. Fargo, I can summon the local constabulary."

Fargo waved off the suggestion and turned away from the desk. His eyes searched the lobby and saw no sign of the woman. Then he recalled that the bar had another entrance on the side of the hotel. Maybe the woman had come in there.

He walked into the bar and looked around. There were a few women in the room, but all of them were with male companions and looked as if they had been there for a while. He realized he didn't really know what the young woman he had rescued looked like. He had never gotten a good look at her.

With a shake of his head, Fargo left the bar and headed across the lobby to the dining room. Whatever was going on, it wasn't really any of his business.

Of course, that had never stopped him from getting mixed up in fracases before. . . .

He found a table in the dining room, dropped his hat in an empty chair, and ordered a steak with all the fixin's from the waiter. A minute later, the waiter returned with the pot of coffee that Fargo had also ordered and poured a cup so that Fargo could sip the strong black brew while he waited for his food.

As Fargo sipped the coffee, he wondered if the local law had come to see what all the commotion was in front of the Alamo. Likely someone had reported the gunshots.

The authorities would find the body of the dead man. But there was nothing to tie Fargo to the corpse, unless the hotel clerk reported that he had come in looking for a possibly frightened young woman. That might be enough for the local badge-toters to connect Fargo to the shooting.

He would cross that bridge when and if he came to it, he told himself. Right now he just wished that steak would hurry up.

Before the food arrived, a burly, white-haired man with a sweeping brush of a mustache came into the dining room and looked around. He had a badge pinned to the lapel of his dusty black coat. Fargo wasn't surprised when the man's searching gaze found him.

The lawman walked across the room and stopped on the other side of the table. "You Fargo?" he asked curtly.

"That's right." Fargo pushed his half-full coffee cup aside. "What can I do for you, Marshal?"

"Tell me what you got to do with a fella layin' over yonder in front of the Alamo, shot plumb full of holes."

Fargo gestured toward the chair. "Have a seat, Marshal. I don't know much more about it than you do, but I'll tell you what I know."

The marshal considered for a second, then nodded in agreement and sank into the chair. "Don't normally sit down at the table with folks I'm questionin', but I could use a cup of coffee right about now."

Fargo grinned and quirked a finger at the waiter, pointing to his cup and then at the marshal. The waiter was watching, of course. Practically everyone in the dining room took an interest in the lawman. They had heard the shots outside a short time earlier.

"What brings you to me, Marshal?" Fargo asked.

"Ed Downey, the clerk out in the lobby, says you were

outside when that ruckus went on and that you came in right after that lookin' for a gal who might be scared. It don't take much thinkin' to figure out that you must know something about what happened." The lawman poured coffee into the cup the waiter placed in front of him. "Downey said you was the only fella in here wearin' buckskins. Name of Fargo." The marshal's eyes, deep-set under bushy white brows, narrowed. "Wouldn't be Skye Fargo, would it?"

"It would."

"The Trailsman."

Fargo inclined his head in acknowledgment of the nickname that had been pinned on him.

"Tell me about that shootin'." The marshal sipped his coffee.

"The dead man had three bullet holes in him. I'm responsible for only one of them, the one in his leg."

"Who put the other two in him?"

"Some hombre who was supposed to be his partner." Quickly, in a low voice that wouldn't be overheard at the other tables, Fargo explained what had happened, not holding back anything. He made it a habit to cooperate with the law whenever he could.

"You didn't know the woman?" the marshal asked when Fargo was finished.

"I still don't. I might not know her if she walked into the dining room right now. I only saw her face for a second as she went through the lobby, and that was from the side."

"If she's a stranger to you, why'd you help her out?" The marshal lifted a hand to forestall an answer. "Never mind, I reckon I know. Most gents out here just naturally try to look out for womenfolks."

Fargo nodded. "Exactly. I didn't like the looks of the men following her."

The marshal sighed. "I don't like corpse and cartridge sessions in my town. San Antonio's an old city, been civilized for a long time. I figure to keep it that way."

"I can sympathize, Marshal, but I felt like I had to take a hand in the game, whatever it was."

"Expect I'd've done the same thing in your place, son."

The lawman drained the last of the coffee from his cup and then shoved his chair away from the table. "You'll be around for the inquest tomorrow morning?"

"I'm not planning on going anywhere," Fargo said truthfully. He had plenty of money at the moment, and the prospect of lazing around San Antonio for a few weeks, playing cards and sipping good whiskey and maybe making the acquaintance of a few of the pretty senoritas, appealed to him quite a bit.

The marshal nodded and left the hotel dining room. When he was gone, the waiter brought over a platter with Fargo's supper on it. Fargo dug in with gusto. Trouble seldom ruined his appetite.

If it had, he reckoned he would have starved to death before now.